COVEN MITT

A WIDOW'S BAY NOVEL

REBECCA REGNIER

CHAPTER 1

I wasn't sure about this plan. Not in the slightest bit. But here I was, sitting around the cauldron with my freshly minted coven.

Pauline, Fawn, Georgie, Tatum, and I had been summoned by Candy. She was agitated, frustrated, and as unhinged as she allowed herself to get.

Excluding of course the time she had that horrifying vision at Lottie Bradbury's casket. Other than that, and it was a big meltdown, Candy didn't give in to emotional scenes. She was a politician, and she was careful to stay nice, calm and politically correct. It was strange for Candy to be this visibly shaken. Her hair was still perfect though.

Strange was the theme for my life lately.

Divorce, career change, a move back to my hometown, surviving being smothered by a homicidal drug addict, and kissing a vampire were just a few of the things going on in my life these days. I was also trying to pick paint colors for my kitchen so yeah, crazy busy.

All of this was in the last few weeks.

I had also refused to mentally unpack the fact that I'd

witnessed a werewolf funeral ritual. I may have an empty nest these days, but I had a packed life.

I'd discovered this new chaos was the key to enjoying my recently roomy nest.

I was also still adjusting to the fact that my old hometown, Widow's Bay, formerly quiet, haunted, and probably cursed, was now bustling, hip, and overrun with vampires, shifters, and trolls. Also, tourists who liked skiing and ancient pagan holidays. We had all that and a kick-ass microbrewery.

The legendary witchy tales that people liked to whisper around a campfire by the lake, about this spooky little corner of the Upper Peninsula were now the town's biggest selling point. A plan conceived and executed by the women in the room with me now. They'd all been recently widowed or divorced, like me, and they'd used their new singlehood to bring life and the undead to our local, flagging, economy.

Still, with all her success and competency, Council Woman Candy Hitchcock was coming unhinged.

"One negative story after another." Candy paced behind us as we warmed ourselves around the cauldron at Tatum's Frog Toe Inn.

It was December.

And in the Upper Peninsula that meant full-on winter. We were hardy up here, and even in December, if the temperature hit freezing you'd see men in cargo shorts at the hardware store.

We'd bypassed nip in the air stage and moved into cold as a witch's, uh, you get the idea. Snow flurries floated in the air, almost all the time. Though the lake wasn't frozen yet, it was on the way.

There were still a few touches of autumn as red and gold leaves held on for dear life as frost and a few inches of snow tried to choke them out. Winter hovered above the gray clouds. It would descend for good soon.

The air was
mountain of whit

Luckily the mi
it was a weeknigh
layers of my swea
sweater. It would be
the subject at hand.

We were gathered
Widow's Bay was ne
coming up in February
direction of public opin
of reassuring her.

"None of the negative
U.P. News." It was the trut
written about Candy. Ev ... ... campaign for Mayor of
Widow's Bay had hit some major snags.

"No legitimate outlet would print the trash they're saying,
Candy," Pauline reassured our friend. She and Candy were the
reason the town was on the uptick as far as I could see. Pauline's
real estate business was booming as a result.

"Be that as it may her campaign should be crushing it right
now. She orchestrated the All Souls Festival, she helped pave the
way for the ski resort, and she's got great outfits!" Georgianne
pointed out all of Candy's strengths. Candy squeezed Georgianne's shoulder in thanks.

"So why am I hearing talk in the waiting room at the clinic
and Tatum's hearing it here at the brewery too. The gossip isn't
great." Fawn added, and Candy looked at me and raised her
eyebrows.

"See, rumors can RUIN this for me." Candy threw her hands
in the air.

"It's just gossip, right?" I asked, but I'd forgotten how small
Widow's Bay was.

"They're saying she was unfaithful to Larry, God Rest His

r idea, well the trip anyway.
phen Brule to get him to open
robably got some side deal with the
hat she hosts those LuLaLa legging
ed the various gossip swirling around

gging thing, that's the one I'd worry about. Those
e paper. Terrible," Georgianne added. The assem-
n agreed the expensive leggings were a crime against
pants.

Candy deserved to be mayor of Widow's Bay. She'd spent her life here making it a better place. She'd worked harder than anyone in town to bring jobs, improve education at the school, to beautify, and to hire new police officers.

"We all know you'd never be caught dead in leggings outside the gym Candy, so that's b.s. but I can't deal in the other rumors. I'm a journalist, we do facts."

"Finding out who started a rumor in this town is like figuring out which snowflake fell first," Tatum said.

"There is a way," Georgianne said. I dreaded where this was going.

"We did it before, and we had no idea what we were up to. Now, imagine, with all six of us," Tatum added.

"This is different though, we were helping the boys score touchdowns, giving them a little push so to speak. For this, we'd be trying to track down gossip." Fawn pointed out the issue but seemed more intrigued than daunted by the prospect.

While I was away in the big city, my friends used our growing powers, to help their kids do well in sports. It was against the witch rules, we'd come to find out, but the state championships were all water under the bridge at this point. I too had used my powers, mostly to smite my cheating ex and his girlfriend. But still, they were all petty reasons to harness elemental forces and what not. We were all trying to do better.

4

"I'll look it up," Georgianne said. Her bookstore and deer processing business, The Broken Spine, was the source of most of our information on the history of Widow's Bay. She also had spell books, local mythology, and the latest Liane Moriarty, so it was well stocked.

"We're talking about casting a spell?" I was equal parts interested and terrified.

"Yep, it's good for Widow's Bay to have a fair and honest election. So, we're going to make sure whoever's trying to stop that gets outed. It's our civic duty," Pauline's eyes sparkled with the idea. It was also good for Pauline's real estate business if the town continued to expand.

"Don't worry Marzie, we're not going to turn anyone into a newt," Tatum said and stood up to head back to work behind the bar.

"Unless they deserve it," Fawn said which elicited a laugh from my friends.

"Oh, God." I put my head in my hands.

"Loosen up, you need to visit your Aunt. It's time you get more detail on how we all fit into this Yooper Natural invasion." Georgie was right.

My Aunt could both clarify and terrify on the subject of vampires, shifters and witch magic. And it was witch magic that we were about to try to deploy.

We needed a better fix on what that might cost us.

The days of me waffling on my role, or magic, or what was really going on in Widow's Bay were over. I was knee deep in all of it.

I may be brand new to witchcraft, wizardry, and dating.

But here I was.

CHAPTER 2

The next morning, I was in my office. I was the only reporter based in Widow's Bay. I'd added a coffee maker, a microwave, and a plant since taking over the Your U.P. News Widow's Bay Bureau. It had quickly become my home away from home. The Old School House Commons office complex, a school that had been converted by Pauline, was the perfect little hub for my new career. I'd quickly come to love the brick building, the wood floors, the hodgepodge of small businesses, and my little window that looked out over Main Street.

I'd spent my life as a reporter and news anchor in the big city of Detroit. But the small town of Widow's Bay was my beat now. And to my surprise, I loved the ability to make my own decisions on stories. I loved that I never knew what the day would bring. I loved the weird and mystical little town that always offered up people and stories that were just as compelling as the ones I'd covered in the big city.

To that end, I perused my calendar for ideas on what to cover. I hoped to swing by a meeting tonight that caught my eye.

I'd heard that the Upper Peninsula Bigfoot/Sasquatch Research Society was in an uproar. I aimed to find out why. My assignment editor, at the main news room, told me readers loved the eccentric stories I found. Luckily, they were a daily occurrence in my small town.

Your U.P. News was an online newspaper. I had found that I didn't miss the television news job in the slightest. Nor did I miss hair, makeup, and teeth whitening on the regular.

Agnes, my judgmental cat, alerted me when I let the grooming slide too far into old hag territory.

"A good white strip on the way to work wouldn't kill you." That was her latest pronouncement.

I drank too much coffee, and Agnes let me know it showed. I didn't tell her that I'd followed her advice and drove the quick commute from my house to the Old School House Commons office building with a tooth whitening strip shakily in place. It felt foreign, and I had to actively manage my gag reflex, but hey, it was for beauty and to shut Agnes up. So, I suffered through it.

I made a point of not lifting my head up on the way into the building for fear of revealing my vanity. With my old job vanity was a job requirement; here, it was not quite a sin, but at least it was something you had the sense to hide a little.

I brewed a morning pot of java in my little office coffee maker. While I waited, I contemplated how long I could stand to have that white strip on. I also started to think about just what story I'd work on today. I typically tried to file a couple a day.

I opened the police scanner app on my phone and listened in.

I didn't expect much, it felt like a quiet morning.

I was wrong.

"Mary Jo, you'll need to dispatch the dive team unit." It was Officer Byron DeLoof. Dive teams? That meant something was underwater somewhere.

I listened a beat more, whatever DeLoof was working on was worth checking, especially if they were going underwater.

I tried to figure out where they were, but I'd missed the original call. I waited a second so Mary Jo, the police department receptionist, could carry out DeLoof's request. And then I called her.

"WBPD." She answered on the first ring.

"Hey Mary Jo, they're requesting a dive team? Where's that address?"

"Yeah, 1256 Whitefish Trail. Submerged vehicle. Seewhy Pond."

"That's out by the farms?"

"Yep."

"Thanks, Mary Jo."

If you asked a police receptionist what's going on, you got nothing. Zero. Bupkis. But if you asked a specific question and had some information already, they almost always gave you more. This was true whether it was Detroit or Widow's Bay. I always got a lot farther when I started with a kernel of something.

Fishing with no bait never yielded results.

I grabbed my bag and locked my office. I wanted to move fast. The key to getting good pictures and details on breaking news was being there as it unfolded, not after.

On my way to Seewhy Pond, and maybe the day's story, I dialed into my main newsroom.

"Newsroom."

Justin Lemorre, my assignment editor, answered. He was young, aggressive and probably wouldn't be in the backwater of news for too long. That was the way of it. You started small and got big, or you started big and got burned out. I was of the burned-out variety.

Our newsroom headquarters were in Sault St. Marie. An hour away, it was the closest big city. Big city was a relative term since Widow's Bay had three traffic lights.

"Morning Justin."

"Morning."

I was gaining confidence as a reporter here with this online news organization. I relished our morning calls. I liked surprising Justin with my story ideas. And he liked my scoops. It made us both look good to our big boss, Garrett DeWitt, the owner of Your U.P. News.

DeWitt had personally congratulated me on the recent murder investigation scoop I'd covered. And on my exclusive interview with the mysterious investor into all things Widow's Bay, Stephen Brule, a.k.a. Etienne Brule.

I hadn't written any stories on who Brule really was. That would veer from fact into fantasy in most readers' eyes. And I'd be out of a job, I was sure of that. If my bosses knew I believed Brule was legendary explorer Etienne Brule, and immortal, and a damn fine kisser, I'd be fired. I tried to go light on coverage of the Yooper Naturals because honestly, you had to see it to believe it anyway.

Nope, just the non-supernatural facts ma'am made it into my reports.

Even so, right now, thanks to my early success, I could pretty much pick what I wanted to cover.

"Widow's Bay PD just called for a dive team."

"Yeah, just heard that on the scanner as well."

"I'm headed out there."

"Okay, let me know as soon as you know."

"Of course."

My Jeep Wrangler was my mobile office. I loaded it with everything I needed. I could pretty much do everything from my Jeep, work-wise.

My trusty four-wheel-drive handled the couple inches of snow well as I made my way about town. The snow cover was good news for business owners and chamber of commerce types since there they were pushing hard to lure skiers, snowboarders, snowshoers, and snowmobilers to town.

If winter wonderland sprinkled with Celtic folklore continued to be a draw for tourists Widow's Bay was all set. The snow was a welcome relief for a town that had hitched its wagon to the new ski resort.

Seewhy Pond was on the farthest outskirts of the township. I checked my phone. It was also next to McGowan Farm.

Tatum was a McGowan by marriage, so I had some idea where I was going. Though it had been years since I'd been out this way.

My phone buzzed as I drove out of town toward the potential breaking news.

It was Georgie.

"Hey, Marzie. What are you working on today?"

"Going out to a water rescue? Maybe?"

"On the lake? What idiot would be boating right now?"

"No, in the pond, Seewhy Pond."

"What's happening out there?"

"No idea yet, but Loof just requested a dive team, that's never good."

"Yikes. Hey, I found some good stuff about our upcoming spell. That's why I called. You're going to have to concoct the words. That's how it works I think."

"Yeah? Okay. But can we talk about that later?"

"Sure, not too much later or Candy's campaign might not survive."

"Something new?"

"Yeah, there's a rumor going around that she bought a Toyota." In Michigan, buying a Japanese car didn't fly if you were running for office. Even though it was impossible to tell what part of your car was made where these days. Detroit was six hours away, heck, a world away as far as I was concerned, but the auto industry was the beating heart of just about everyone in Michigan. Buying a foreign car, if you were running for office, wasn't the way to get elected.

"Ew, yeah, well, let me know when we're, uh, getting together for, ah, it." I couldn't say casting, I couldn't say cauldron, I couldn't say magic. Even though that's exactly what we were about to attempt.

"I will, I think Fawn will have to get us hair of…"

"I'm going to interrupt you. I can't mix spell casting and fact gathering. New research says multi-tasking is bad for productivity."

"Chicken. Talk to you later."

"Right, try not to unleash ancient homicidal mummies or similar with your research."

"You're no fun." We hung up. I was only half kidding. Who knew what we were about to conjure?

I focused on the task at hand. And slowed down when I started to see activity. I hadn't even used the GPS! I was getting better at remembering where everything was in Widow's Bay. Though it wasn't hard to spot the pond I was looking for. Red lights on official vehicles had the place lit up like a Christmas display.

I slowed down as I approached.

Emergency vehicles gathered around the pond. In the distance there was a farmhouse, I thought it was Earl McGowan's but twenty years away from Widow's Bay made my mastery of every location somewhat shaky.

I was getting better though. Earl McGowan was Tatum's father-in-law. If she talked about him at all, "grumpy old bastard" was the phrase she used, instead of loving grandpa. I didn't relish knocking on his door and asking for his reaction to all the activity.

It was a rarity to see a lot of open space in Widow's Bay unless you were on the shore of Lake Superior. Lush forest, a rugged mountain peak, and the glistening lakes made for some picture postcard vistas around here. But open farmland, like you'd find downstate, was a lot less common. This was a patch of farm in a place where farming was hard as hell.

Officer Byron DeLoof was in charge of the scene. I snapped a few pictures for the paper. A police vehicle and a water rescue team from the fire department were working near the water.

Now that I was here, I could see a vehicle was in the water. It was front end down. The back end was just barely visible.

Firefighters were securing a line to the back bumper of a pickup truck. The bumper had just broken the surface of the water. There were icy patches on the pond, but it hadn't frozen solid yet.

"Hey Marzie, hope you've got layers. The wind's picking up." And it was. The December air could be mistaken for February. I shuddered when I thought about what actual February would be like. It had been a long time since I'd stayed up here for more than a few days of winter.

"What can you tell me?" I nodded towards the pond.

"The pond level is low this morning. A couple of drivers spotted the tail light reflectors."

"Why is it low? We're not in a drought, and we've got snow?"

"No idea?"

"This is McGowan's, right?"

"Yep, that's McGowan's Farm, we're just at the edge of his place."

"Earl McGowan lives alone out here right?"

"Yeah."

"Is he home?"

"Nope, no answer up at the house. We need to back up a bit." Loof put a hand on my arm and guided me backward a few steps in the snow.

"Hit it!" One of the rescue team members yelled. The line they'd hooked to the back of the truck pulled tight as the rescue vehicle slowly drove farther away from the pond.

"Any of the people who called it in around?" I asked, hoping to interview someone other than authorities, or Earl McGowan. My choices were going to be limited since the closest house to McGowan's farm was acres away.

Slowly, the truck emerged from the pond. A thin layer of ice that had coated the surface cracked and shifted as more of the truck was hauled up.

"You might not want to look," Loof cautioned me.

"Why? A soggy old pick up isn't pretty, but I think I can handle it."

"It's a soggy old Earl I'm worried you're not going to want to see."

As he said it the vehicle was hauled completely out of the water and to the bank of the pond. The crew ordered a halt to the towing.

A FIREFIGHTER WALKED AROUND to the front and gave the driver side door a tug. Water rushed out.

I strained around Loof to see. There was someone in the driver's seat. Oh boy.

"You knew?"

"Yeah, the dive team said the driver was still strapped in. Way too late to rescue, all recovery this morning."

"Ah, and is that Earl?"

"Let's see," DeLoof said as he walked forward toward the scene. I wasn't one to be waved off a story, so I followed.

It was a man's body. He was slight, and wore a flannel shirt and jeans. A few wispy hairs covered his otherwise bald head. His head, hands, and face were tinged bluish white. The corpse looked more soggy than frozen.

"I'd say whoever it is, it's been under water a few weeks," DeLoof said.

"Is it Earl? Can I name him for my story?"

"It looks Earlesque to me, but I gotta call Tatum. She'll have to i.d. him. She's the only family he has, and I don't think they speak."

"That's sad."

DeLoof surveyed the scene, and I stopped asking questions. I wanted him to forget I was there so I wouldn't get kicked out.

I walked around the area and tried to picture what might have happened.

The driveway to the McGowan farmhouse was visible up the road. Had the dead man made a wrong turn? If it was Earl I had to figure he knew the place back and forth; he'd lived here his entire life. Maybe he had a heart attack? Maybe he was confused in his old age?

I took a few more photos from a respectful distance.

After a few minutes, I walked back to Loof.

"Okay, we need to do a quick interview. Then I'll let you go."

"Budd hates when I do this."

"It's this, or I camp out at his office all day. He likes that even less."

Chief Budd Marvin had never submitted to an interview by me. I hadn't been reporting in Widow's Bay for long, but it was easy to see if I wanted information it was always Loof, not his boss who'd get it for me.

I fired my questions at Loof. He liked to liberally sprinkle his interview answers with cop jargon for no reason other than he thought it sounded official.

"Loof! You're going to want to see this." One of the fire crew guys waved Loof over before I'd finished asking questions.

"I've got to get back to it Marzie."

"Sure, I'll call you later with follow-ups."

I watched for a moment more as they laid the body in a tarp.

The coroner van arrived.

That was a sure sign that things were wrapping up here. If I hurried, I could knock on one door and get this written before the lunch hour. Web traffic on Your U.P. News spiked during the lunch break. Justin liked having fresh stories for people scrolling through the site while they ate their lunch.

I took one more long look at the scene. Earl McGowan's farm

could well have been Siberia. Powdery snow covered the ground. The cold wind lifted it like dry sand. The white salt-like powder swirled over the expanse of field. The old farmhouse stood alone, empty, and dark, and at least an acre away from Seewhy Pond.

I wondered how Tatum would take the news. It was a terrible thing to have to ID a body even if that body wasn't your favorite person.

I looked at the tracks on the driveway. Footprints had been the key that unlocked the last suspicious death in Widow's Bay.

The treads of the emergency vehicles were a mix of mud and snow, it was the consistency of mashed potatoes and gravy. Footprints and tire tracks ran together. The emergency workers treated this as a rescue at first, and that meant speed, not evidence preservation, was vital when they first drove in.

I walked back to the Jeep.

I was thankful for my four-wheel drive again. I couldn't wait to blast the heater to try to recover from the time outside in the cold. I looked down at my boots. They were coated in mud and snow.

I leaned down and grabbed the roll of paper towels that I kept on the passenger side floor. I tried to keep my mobile office clean. It was a losing battle.

As I swiped a layer off my boots, I realized something was stuck to the side of one. I peeled off a disc, the size of a silver dollar that had gotten wedged in between the sole and the upper of the thick tread boots I now wore as part of my uniform.

"What the heck is this?" I turned the muddy little piece of plastic over. How'd that get stuck to me? Well, it was better than dog doo, or cow manure, all of which were possibilities out here.

I deposited the little disk in a wad of the paper towels I'd amassed to try to clean up. I had a nice little mess on my passenger side floor that I was quite sure needed to be dealt with if Agnes would ever deign to ride in the Jeep again.

I also realized if anyone were kind enough to open the door

to a reporter today I'd have to stay on the porch. It just wasn't polite to track mud into a person's home. Especially if you were asking them for a favor, like giving you a quote.

I looked around.

Earl McGowan had precisely one neighbor. Time to do some legwork.

Earl's lone neighbor was a farmer named Bertrand Lasko. I knocked on his door in hopes I could flesh out more about Earl McGowan and when he was last seen.

Lasko answered his door; he had to be at least as old as Earl. He had a look of someone not used to having company on the front porch.

"Hi Mr. Lasko, I'm Marzie Nowak, a reporter for Your U.P. News. I'm trying to get a reaction to the commotion there at the pond on your neighbor's property. Wondered if you could remember when you last saw Earl McGowan?"

"Is he dead? Was it him in the pond? Oh my, I'll pray right now. He was a fine man, such a good neighbor!"

"I'm so sorry. It's not confirmed. I wouldn't want to give you the wrong information until it's official. But, uh you were close? When did you see him last?"

My questions were left unfinished as Bertrand Lasko slammed the screen door in my face.

Grief affects people in different ways. Clearly, Bertrand Lasko was so overcome with emotion over the idea that Earl McGowan might be dead, that speaking had become impossible.

I walked back to my Jeep. I felt terrible for the old farmer, both of them truth be told.

I filed the story from my Jeep office.

Man found dead in truck submerged in frigid pond

Widow's Bay, MI

Widow's Bay Police are investigating the discovery of a body found in a truck submerged in the pond near McGowan Farm.

"We received a call from a civilian motorist that they'd observed tail

light reflectors in the small body of water," said Officer Byron DeLoof of the Widow's Bay Police Department.

The fire department deployed its water rescue team.

"We had hoped we were on a rescue mission, but it was quickly determined that there was a deceased body in the vehicle and rescue would not be possible," DeLoof added.

The incident unfolded shortly before seven a.m.

Authorities could not speculate how long the body and the vehicle had been submerged in the pond. They say a forensic pathology exam is required to positively identify the victim.

"It appears this vehicle has been submerged for a couple of weeks. We'll need to lean on the pathologist's exam to be sure there's no foul play here," DeLoof explained.

The Michigan State Police Crime Lab in Marquette has been alerted and will perform the examination.

"It could be a little while before we have a positive identification or a definitive cause of death."

Authorities wouldn't speculate on whether it was a crime or an accident.

The area of Widow's Bay is sparsely populated. The few nearby residents told police they did not notice anything suspicious over the last few weeks.

Your U.P. News will update this story as new details become available.

CHAPTER 3

"*I*t's him."

Tatum took all of three seconds to look at the photo Loof presented to her.

"We all thought so, but you have to make it official."

"Does she have to do the whole morgue thing?"

"No, we're good. Unless you want to."

"Yeah right Loof that sounds great. I can't wait!"

"Uh well," Loof shifted from one foot to the other.

"I'm kidding. If this is good for you, it's good for me."

I'd met Tatum at the police department. I didn't want her to have to do this alone. Even if Earl McGowan wasn't on her Christmas list these days, it was still hard.

"You okay?"

"Yeah, I'm fine. I hadn't seen him in years, he didn't even come to Pat's memorial service. His own son. Pat said the man never did anything but swing a belt around him."

"I'm sorry."

"Well, that's why we married young, we wanted out of our parents' houses."

"So, any idea how his truck wound up in the pond?" I wondered if we had a murder or an accident on our hands. I was here as a friend for Tatum but still, may as well see if there was an update.

"No, not yet," Loof said.

"Can we go?" Tatum asked, and Loof nodded.

"Safe to say the relatives are informed, and the body is Earl McGowan's?"

"Yes, official," Loof added. Tatum and I walked out of the Widow's Bay Government Center. The Barrel, as locals called it, housed just about all the government offices from local to state in these parts. The natural distrust of government helped the building earn its nickname, as in pork barrel. Though the two government employees I knew well, Loof and Candy, worked their butts off for the people.

"When was the last time you saw Earl?" I asked Tatum as we walked to my car.

"Jeez, other than the random encounter in town? Had to be over fifteen years. He showed up drunk at Zack's flag football game once."

"Wow, that's awful."

"He started complaining that they weren't tackling. Mind you, I said flag football. Something about how it looked more like a ballet recital. Anyway, yeah, a real gem that Earl McGowan. Pat wound up practically punching him in the face to get him out of there."

"His wife died when Pat was in High School?"

"Yep, really my Zachary is the only blood relative left. I'm going to call him now, let him know. I think he'll be okay. But, still."

"Yeah, still. I'll keep on Loof for the investigation. I'll update you as we go. Hey, want to get some lunch?"

"No, I gotta get back to the lunch rush myself." Tatum worked hard running the Frog Toe. I wondered how she did it some days. Her compact muscles were evidence that hoisting a keg around was a good workout.

"Got it."

"And we're doing the spell tomorrow night. I had time this morning, so I've already started the brew."

"Are we really doing this?"

"Are you really asking? Of course, we are. Candy deserves to be mayor even if she is a tight ass. She's the best thing for the future of Widow's Bay."

"That's true."

"Bring your magic words." Tatum gave me a quick hug and dashed off.

Magic words. That was up to me, the words to the actual spell. I had no idea how to create one. I'd only intentionally done magic once. And that was to save my own life. I had summoned help from Stephen AKA Etienne Brule when I was trouble. It was a life and death thing, and I reacted. It worked, and Brule sent help.

Every other time I'd done something magical it was an accident. It was my will or desire making something happen, like my ex getting a boil on his face, or his mistress falling on her rear end. I wasn't sure how to go about conjuring a spell to reveal who was starting the rumors against Candy.

But I knew someone who did, Aunt Dorothy.

I called my ancient aunt, but she didn't answer. Instead, a text arrived, complete with smiling emojis.

"What's up Butter Cup?" Came the text answer.

"I need to meet you, I have questions."

"Fine, busy, but pick me up at my house, you can run an errand with the ladies and me. They're already here."

"On the way."

I drove to my Aunt's house. I worried that it might be too big for her, now that I realized she was probably over 100 years old. But she loved it, managed it, and seemed not to be bothered by the stairs to the three floors.

Three ladies greeted me at the door. Frances Corey and Maxine Proctor, along with my Aunt Dorothy Nurse, were the last of the Widow's Bay Distinguished Ladies Club. If Brule, Dorothy, and the old documentation that Georgie found were to be believed, they were all three descended from the witches of Salem. Which meant I was too. Something I still couldn't wrap my head around.

"You're really looking so much younger now that you're back home!" Frances complimented me. I could say the same about her and the other two ladies. They were 100 plus but looked barely seventy.

I had no idea why she thought I was looking younger. I had let a gray streak, that had appeared after my near-death experience, grow at my temple. I was confident that if I were still a television news anchor, it would be grounds for dismissal. In Widow's Bay, it was barely a blip.

"I have no make-up on, my hair is windblown, and my jeans are all muddy. How do you figure that, Frances?"

"Those are exactly the things that make you look beautiful! Plus, kissing Etienne, that had to add a little pep in your step."

"That's none of your business, get in the Jeep." At times Frances' psychic ability could be very unnerving.

"Oh, I didn't know you kissed him!" Aunt Dorothy was about to pump me for details, no psychic abilities needed for that prediction.

"Oh, there's a mess of towels here." Maxine pointed out the mess that I'd left on the Jeep floor from my morning story.

"I need to clean up the car a bit. I didn't realize I'd be driving the remnants of the Distinguished Ladies Club around town today."

I shoved the mess to the side to make way for the trio of Dorothy, Frances, and Maxine.

I helped the ladies situate themselves in my Jeep.

"Okay, ladies, where to?"

"We're headed to the Ulmer house."

"Help me out here?"

"Oh, the Ulmers live in that subdivision, Tituba Woods."

I knew the place.

"So, what was your question? How can we help you, Marzenna?" Aunt Dorothy asked.

I had a lot of questions. Thanks to Georgie's research we'd learned that the women of Widow's Bay had made a pact, long ago, with Etienne Brule and other supernaturals, now coined Yooper Naturals by Dorothy and her friends. And when I say long ago, I'm talking Mayflower long. Before there was a U.S.A., there was Widow's Bay.

Thanks to this pact, women here had safety, liberty, agency, and positions of power, hundreds of years before women anywhere else in this country. But they paid for it by hiding the Yooper Naturals, which so far, in my experience, included vampires, werewolves, bear shifters, and trolls. This, I was told, just scratched the surface. A point I hadn't yet delved into too deeply.

My sense of skepticism required visual confirmation and what I'd seen so far had overloaded my circuit boards. There was no need to hunt for evidence of the rest of the pantheon of monsters. The way things were going in my life, I'd wind up in a Pilates class with them by the end of the week.

"We're going to be trying a spell, my friends and me."

"It better not be one to help win football games, that's just frivolous." Maxine piped up from the back seat.

"No, it's to see who's running a smear campaign against Candy in her mayoral race."

"Oh, good, that's a good reason then." Magic approved by Maxine, what could go wrong?

"Unless you can just see it?" I asked Frances, maybe we didn't need to tinker with spells if Frances's powers could do the trick. I like that idea.

"Nothing so far has popped into my head?" Frances added after a thoughtful look up to the roof of the Jeep.

"It's excellent dear, that Candy should be mayor, she reminds me of me, way more than you do."

Aunt Dorothy had been mayor, back in her heyday, and it was true, she had a penchant for organizing meetings, people, and Tupperware. Just like Candy did.

I never wanted to run the town or a television station or anything. I was always driven to find stories and share them. Journalism was my calling, not campaigning.

"You know you need three, right?" Maxine asked me, and I nodded. That much we'd discovered on our own. When three of us or more were together, we were powerful. We had magic on our own, magic we were just learning to use. But as a group, we'd been accidentally or on purpose able to do things, unexplainable things, since middle school.

"You'll all have a part to play. I think Georgianne found that out for you, didn't she?" Aunt Dorothy asked.

"Yes, she had the elements, or finds them in her books, Fawn brings things from animals or nature, Tatum minds the brew, Candy seems to function as some sort of focus for us, and I have no idea what Pauline's role is."

"Neither do I. No hurry, it will come to her. It took Jane a while to figure out, remember that, Maxine?" Most of Dorothy's contemporaries were gone. Jane Parrish died of a heart attack, Elsie had an aneurysm, and Lottie was murdered. There were only three left now of the core group of the DLC. They'd lived a long time, longer than anyone would believe, but they were dwindling, and that's where my generation was supposed to step up to the plate.

We were trying. But it wasn't like you could take an online class on spell casting and get certified. What we needed to learn we needed to learn from Dorothy, and by trial and error. Which was where I got very nervous. I didn't want to error. It wasn't like bouncing a check or missing a step at Zumba. I had no idea how powerful we were or the consequences of that power.

My first real immersion into Widow's Bay was uncovering the story of an angry witch who killed a bus full of husbands in a quest for more power. Not exactly something you put on the brochure for students in the market for an associate's degree in witchcraft.

"We're going to be doing a spell on Pam Ulmer. This will be perfect. You can watch," Aunt Dorothy said.

"Why?"

"Oh, well, she's a little older than you, not much, anyway we suspect she's come into her full power, and she's abusing it," Aunt Dorothy went on.

"Abusing it? She's not hurting anyone, is she? Like Lottie did?"

"Lottie killed people to increase her power. That was drastic, evil, and not at all what we stand for," Frances said.

"We're also not here to waste our talents on petty things, like how your friends were fixing the football games, and improving the landscaping of real estate properties they were trying to sell." That had to have been Pauline's doing. She'd do anything to close a deal.

"What's Pam doing then?"

"Best you just hover back, watch, and learn. If we speak it now, we could inadvertently tip her off," Aunt Dorothy said.

"So, just bring up the rear?" I asked.

"Yep, and hold my purse, I have mints in there, and sometimes you just need one after, you know?" Aunt Dorothy said. The ladies nodded in knowing agreement. I knew my face was full on resting witch as I considered the shenanigans I was sure I was about to witness.

"We're here!" Maxine pointed to the house. Dorothy handed me her purse. I followed Dorothy, Maxine, and Frances up to Pam Ulmer's front door, and Dorothy rang the bell.

CHAPTER 4

*N*o answer, though I could hear a baby crying and some shuffling inside the home.

"Did you hear that?" Dorothy asked. Frances and Maxine nodded.

"Her baby's crying. Maybe she has her hands full right now?" I was afraid my nutty trio of old ladies planned to interrupt a busy new mother.

"I'm sure she does," Dorothy said and opened the screen door this time to knock. Loudly.

Finally, the door opened.

"Pam! So good to see you," Dorothy took the opportunity to edge her way into the foyer. Maxine, Frances and I followed.

"Dorothy! Ladies, I'm so sorry I don't really have time to chat. The house is a mess. I just.."

"What's got you so busy?" Dorothy wasn't one to beat around the bush. Pam Ulmer looked embarrassed and flustered by the question.

I felt bad for her. It was clear, from the diapers, baby toys, and general disarray of the place, that Pam Ulmer was a new mom. I was a new mom in my twenties, I couldn't imagine how trying it would be to do in your forties like Pam. But no matter when you had a newborn it was overwhelming. I had no idea why Dorothy couldn't see that.

"Uh, volunteering, and my online business. I'm selling crafts on Etsy."

"Volunteering where? No one's seen you in almost two months," Dorothy pointed out.

As Dorothy faced down a now frightened Pam, I noticed Maxine encroaching further into the home.

"Hey, I said the house is a mess." She tried to reach out to Maxine who was now strolling around the kitchen.

"Lots of baby bottles in here. Watching a grandchild? I didn't know any of your brood had a little one." Maxine said, as she opened and closed the woman's refrigerator. The Distinguished Ladies Club was utterly intrusive and downright rude.

"Aunt Dorothy, we should go. Clearly Pam is taking care of a newborn. It's stressful enough without unannounced visitors." Pam looked at me with gratitude.

Somehow, without anyone realizing it, Frances had found the newborn and was now cradling it in her arms. Pam was frozen to her spot at the sight.

"Well?" Aunt Dorothy directed the question at Frances.

"Hold on." Frances leaned down and put her forehead on the infant's.

Maxine put a hand on Pam's shoulder.

"Don't worry, this is perfectly safe."

Frances closed her eyes, and we all waited for a few seconds.

"I'll get you out of there. Yep. Just hang on," Frances said to the baby. And then she returned her focus to us. It was all Dorothy needed.

"What were you thinking, dear?" Dorothy directed the question to Pam.

"What? I haven't done anything. I don't know what you're

talking about!" Her eyes betrayed her words. They darted from the baby to the women who now surrounded her.

"That baby is Conner," Frances said.

I was confused; so the baby's name was Conner, big deal.

"It is not, it's my new baby, uh, Seacrest."

"Seacrest? You named him after the host of America n Idol?"

"He's very smooth," Pam defended her name choice.

"It's a lovely name." I tried to diffuse the tension in the room.

"Pam, you had a complete hysterectomy three years ago. Remember, I brought you dinner and set up the Meal Chain Train? If I recall, your youngest baby is eighteen and was supposed to move to college a few months ago. Where was it? I forget."

"Conner got a scholarship to Western Michigan. It was on the fridge." Maxine said and waved a letter in the air.

"That's right, he did great on his ACT test! I remember hearing that," Dorothy added, and Pam was shaking her head no.

Even if the woman had a hysterectomy, this could be adoption, or a surrogate, or a foster. Tears were starting to roll down poor Pam's eyes. Whatever the ladies were a part of right now I wanted out.

Frances looked at me now.

"Honey, Pam cast a spell on her eighteen-year-old son, and well..." she looked down at little Seacrest.

"What?"

"It happens," Maxine said. It happens? What happens? This was nuts.

"Pam, you can tell us. It's okay. We're not mad," Dorothy said. And Pam collapsed to the nearby couch.

"Time was going too fast. I just wanted them all to be little forever. First my girl Paige, and then Timmy left, and I just couldn't do it again." Dorothy sat next to Pam and put an arm around her shoulder.

"There, there. I know."

"I just wanted them to stay little. That's not wrong." Pam said to me this time.

"I do not get it." I was trying to process it.

Maxine came up beside me and whispered an explanation.

"She cast a spell to make her youngest stay little. She was so worried about the whole empty nest thing, she trapped Conner in this baby body."

"Oh, my." Wanting to keep your kids little and actually keeping them little were two different things. The first was what every mom said or thought, once in a while; the second was horrible.

"Conner is ready to return to his normal form. I checked," Frances said to the group.

"Pam, the three of us are going to do this. Go get a blanket. When, uh, baby Seacrest reverts back to Conner his diaper and onesie aren't going to fit."

"I didn't want to hurt anything. I just wanted to keep him a little baby, and cute, and with me. He was my last one. They don't need me when they go to college. I know it was wrong, I know." Pam said, and Dorothy patted her on the shoulder.

I understood now. More than I wanted to admit. I'd felt the same things Pam had felt. I wondered how many moms would have done something like this if they had the power. Seeing how actually twisted it was, well, it would cure anyone from wanting to keep their kids "little forever." There was a man trapped in a baby's body. The very thought made me a little queasy.

"We will fix it dear, and didn't you learn something?" Aunt Dorothy had a stern tone of a teacher right now.

"Yes, I... I really miss Conner. Teenage Conner is so wonderful. I just can't seem to reverse it, the thing I did."

"We're here to help. And you don't have time to care for a baby. We need you for bigger things. Now go get a blanket. Conner is going to be confused at first, let's not traumatize him further by having him wake up naked as a jaybird in front of a room full of strange women."

"Okay, yes, I'll get it right away."

"This is our fault. We should have taken you young ones under our wing from the beginning," Aunt Dorothy said to me.

"What?"

"Pam's spell, her feeling she's not needed. She doesn't realize that she's needed much more now, by all of us, by the town itself, by the Yooper Naturals. Ugh, I was so distracted by Lottie's antics we just didn't do our part for your generation. But, we're on the right track now."

"Ah," It was a weak response, and the only one I could come up with.

"We're going to do the reverse spell. Marzie, just watch, see how it's done. You'll probably have to do it at some point. There's always one mom who just can't leave 'em at the dorm," Dorothy said.

"You'll be better equipped for your spell about Candy after you watch ours," Frances said as she put little Seacrest on the couch.

"Here's the blanket." Pam came over and draped a Green Bay Packers fleece over Seacrest who was kicking his legs around. Frances kept a hand on his chest to be sure he stayed secure on the couch.

"You two stay outside our circle, and we'll be done in no time."

I took Pam's hand, and we did as instructed.

The three living members of the Widow's Bay Distinguished Ladies Club gathered close to the baby. They locked hands.

The room was quiet, and the air was charged with something I couldn't name. It was an energy I recognized but didn't know how to channel or control. The Distinguished Ladies did.

Dorothy spoke, and her voice was strong and deeper than I'd ever heard it. This was a woman in charge.

. . .

Born out of love, but not out of logic.
  Raised to soar, not to swaddle!
  Throw wide the door, cease all the coddle.
  Reverse the spell to keep the last born close.
  He is a man now of 18-years.
  Release him from his mother's fears.

Return Conner to his natural form
  These eighteen years from when he was born.
  Nest be thee empty
  Love still be plenty!

Maxine put the college letter on the baby, and Frances again leaned her head over little Seacrest. Dorothy said the words, Maxine had the item, the letter, and Frances was there, connecting with the subject of their spell. I tried to take it all in. I noted each witch's contribution.

My view of baby Seacrest was somewhat blocked by the circle of biddies around him. I struggled to see.

The form of the baby shimmered. Molecules felt like they were speeding up and shifting all around us. I blinked my eyes and in place of the baby was a teenager.

"Conner!" Pam said, and she broke through the circle of witches to kneel at his side. The little onesie was ripped to shreds, in tatters around Conner's neck.

"It's okay Conner, you're back to your normal form and age," Frances said.

He looked down at his long hairy legs, and at the women in the room.

"Seacrest? You actually renamed me Seacrest?"

"I know, I should have gone with DJ Khalid or the Macklemore guy."

CHAPTER 5

I drove the ladies back to my Aunt's and tried to keep them on task with my line of questions.

"So do you always need the same things? A mental connection, a physical item, like the letter, and then the words to do a spell?"

"No, I mean Pam did pretty well on her own." Aunt Dorothy said. It was true, trapping an eighteen-year-old into the body of a baby seemed rather epic.

"Yes, but that spell was breaking apart, I sensed it in the boy," Frances said.

"The key is that the three witches are on the same page. That you're all bringing your focus to the issue," Maxine said.

"We can't do everything, there are limits. And there are different channels through which our powers flow, your Tatum for instance, that beer she brews, powerful stuff," Aunt Dorothy said.

"And tasty, I had the pale summer ale after weeding the garden, I got the spins," Frances said. These three sober were more than I could handle, buzzed, I didn't even want to think about it.

. . .

"LOTTIE'S REFRIGERATOR was packed with soup when I was at her house. Could that have been something she used to brew her spells?"

"Oh, for sure. She made the worst food. Elsie, rest her soul, tried to teach her how to make it less like slop, but Lottie didn't listen," Maxine said.

"Lottie went rogue, she had to kill to get power, and probably thought she had to brew all that nasty stuff to make her spells work," Frances added.

I had forgotten about finding all the soup until this very conversation.

"I have no doubt you'll all do just fine with your little rumor-mongering spell, it's not too difficult. You'll do the words, Georgianne will be sure to do the research. That combined with Fawn's affinity for animals, Tatum's brew, and Candy's focus. It will be easy!"

"Pauline, she can be the hype girl. That's a thing. I read about it." Frances knew about hype girls? I didn't even know about hype girls.

"What if we mess it up? What are the costs? There have to be costs."

Aunt Dorothy looked at me.

"Your motives are pure, and not selfish. You're undertaking this spell to help the town, Candy is the right person to lead Widow's Bay. Nothing bad will happen. Stop worrying," Aunt Dorothy said as if that ought to put an end to my issues over casting a spell, on purpose, for the first time.

"Well, weren't Pam's motives pure? She loves little Seacrest, or Conner, or whatever."

"Oh, no, caging a person, whether it be with bars or in time, is wrong. And Pam did it for herself, not for the good of her son. But we'll get her right," Aunt Dorothy said, and I couldn't argue.

"I think she's a decent baker, might be useful now that Elsie's gone. We still don't have enough baked goods for the Yule Days," Maxine added.

"Good thinking!"

As I dropped them off the three witches were still planning how best to help Pam snap out of her empty nest depression. Baked goods seemed as good an idea as any.

I was so busy learning about Widow's Bay and Yooper Naturals, that I hadn't thought too much about my own empty nest.

I now lived alone. It was odd, and liberating, and seldom quiet.

And for the first time in my adult life, I was enjoying decorating a house for me. Not for babies, toddlers, football players, gamers, or my husband. Me.

I could actually choose white, or pink, or lemon colored accents. Or, praised be, a floral print.

The reno at my new nest was in full swing. Every day something new was demolished or restored.

I called Loof as I drove home just to see if there was any update on Earl McGowan's death.

"Hey, anything to report?"

"No, probably not until tomorrow morning."

"How long do you think he was in the water? Just a guess. Not for the news."

"It's hard to say, we're pretty sure no one's seen him for over two weeks."

"Do you think he was in the water that long?"

"We noticed the water level on the pond had gone down, that's why someone saw the back of the truck. It was probably totally submerged until this morning."

"Is that normal? The water level going down? We've had a lot of snow, before that, rain."

"I don't know Marzie, I'm a police officer, not a meteorologist."

"Okay, then answer me this, do you know who saw him last?"

"No, not yet, that's what I'm working on while the lab works up the cause of death. He probably stroked out and drove into the pond."

"You think?"

"Most obvious choice is usually the solution. And none of this is in your story right?"

"Nah, I just filed the basics for now. Until tomorrow when you're giving me something more to report."

"You're relentless." We ended the call.

Loof was probably right. Earl most likely died before he hit the water; clogged arteries, bad heart, or any number of things could punch your clock.

I did wonder, why was the pond low? Maybe there was another story there. Perhaps I had some environmental story or weather lead I could track down if nothing new happened. I was always on the hunt for a story to file. Curiosity was key to find the nugget that you could mine for gold. I still couldn't believe how fun it was to pare down from the hype of television news and work for the little online operation. I'd found the perfect job, by accident, after being fired from what I thought was my dream job as a big market television anchor. Six months ago I wouldn't have believed you if you told me that.

Thanks to Loof's comment about meteorologists I remembered I did have access to an expert on why water in the pond could be low despite the amount of snow and rain we'd had.

I dialed my old station, WXYD in Detroit. Elaine, the sweetest receptionist in the world, answered.

"WXYD, Home of Detroit's Action News, how can I help you?"

"Good to hear your voice, Elaine."

"MARZIE! How are you???"

I'd spent years at WXYD, I grew up there, my kids grew up there, and I missed some of the people. Not all of the people, mind you. I did not miss my cheating ex-husband, the main anchor of WXYD, or his girlfriend, the hot new reporter. And I hadn't thought of those two nearly at all after I'd crossed the bridge to the Upper Peninsula and left them downstate. They were the catalyst for my current adventure, so if anything, I owed them thanks.

I hoped the speed in which I adjusted to this new phase of my life was a sign from the universe that I was exactly where I was supposed to be, Yooper Naturals and all.

"I'm great, Elaine, loving life up here in Widow's Bay. You should plan a trip!"

"Oh, I would love that, the snow, the scenery, the pasties!"

To everyone else in the country, a pasty was something a stripper wore. In Northern Michigan, they were a meat concoction wrapped in a delicious pastry pocket.

"They've got this Yule Days thing in a few days, and another one in February. Judging how they did up the fall one, I think you'd love it."

"Oh, if only I had the days off to use."

"I get you. Well, I am fixing up my house and have several extra rooms if you ever want to come!"

"A regular bed and breakfast!"

"Except I can't promise you the breakfast part. Being the lone reporter in town has me pretty busy."

"It sounds divine. We miss you, ratings haven't been the same without you."

"Good, I mean I'm sorry about that for the rest of the station, but for Sam and Kayleigh, well, it does serve them right."

"Oh, they're broken up. Didn't you know?"

"Really? And I thought what they had was the real thing!" I generally tried not to be catty, but Sam brought it out in me.

"Yeah, she's dating one of the Detroit Lions, I forget which one. Left Sam in the dust."

"Ouch."

"Yep, so what can I do for you?"

"Connect me to Dash's line okay?"

"Got a weather question?"

"Yep."

"Well, he's the one to ask. Great talking to you!"

"You too, and remember my place is open. Think about it."

"Will do." Elaine transferred me to Dash Montgomery, Chief Meteorologist for WXYD.

"WXYD Storm Team HQ!" It was Dash himself. Dash was an institution in Detroit television. He'd started at the station in the late seventies. He'd gone from Ron Burgundy looking to Willard Scott looking, and no one ever suggested he Botox or bleach anything. Apparently, an older man was palatable for viewers, a woman over thirty, not so much.

But Dash knew his stuff, he always treated me with respect and had had a unique vantage point to watch Sam and I fight over what was news and what was fluff.

"Hey Dash, I have a climate question for you?"

"Marzie!!!" He had a booming voice, the kind that old school radio announcers would envy.

Dash and I quickly caught up. And then I got into the reason I called. Inland water levels in Chippewa County, Michigan.

There wasn't a reason he could think of why the pond water would be low in the Upper Peninsula after the weather we'd had lately.

"Something other than weather's causing it, Marzie, that's my best estimate. Now I can pull yearly water levels, and look at temperature variations over the last fifty years. There are factors to consider. If there's something else at work, climatologically speaking, you know old Dash will find it!"

"I know, and I appreciate it. No one knows Michigan climate like you, and no one ever will, Dash! I'm more than good for now on this story. Thank you."

"Too kind, talk to you soon."

We hung up, I was nearly back at my house by this point.

I didn't think the pond level had a thing to do with the Earl McGowan story, but maybe there was an environmental story there.

Half of the things I checked on, was curious about, or noticed, never made it into a news story. But my job was to notice and question. I filed away the information about the pond level in the back of my brain. Maybe, on the next slow news day, I'd dig it out again to see if there was something to report.

There was a now familiar truck in my driveway.

My ordinarily quiet house had become quite busy, and I walked into a standoff.

Grady Shook stood in the archway to the dining room with his hands on his hips. The man had the uncanny ability to come to my rescue. The home improvements were no exception.

I'd hired Grady to handle the reno, accidently, sort of.

By trade Grady and a lot of the new residents were loggers, but the logging operation wasn't going full speed yet, and he had downtime.

Grady had seen me post an ad on the Old School House commons job board for a home improvement contractor and showed up with it in his hand. Leaning on Grady had become a habit.

Grady was a sight. Tight shirt, rippling muscles, long thick auburn hair, and sparkling eyes had everyone in our spin class drooling when he showed up the first time. He was also a flirt, with a devastating smile. He just happened to also be a werewolf. Because of course he was, this was Widow's Bay.

"Thank goodness you're here," Grady said as I walked toward my dining room.

Grady had saved me from Kyle Bradbury when he tried to kill me. I was supposed to be magically connected to Stephen nee Étienne Brule, but if stuff went down during the day, Grady was the one who magically appeared.

I didn't know what any of it really meant. Maybe it was best not to analyze. Bottomline Grady was a trustworthy contractor, and currently, my late 1800s Victorian painted lady needed more rescuing than I did. Everywhere else in suburbia, finding a good contractor was as rare as running into a werewolf. In Widow's Bay, you had your pick of both.

"I was going to say the same to you." Grady was working on removing the carpet in the entire first floor. He had accurately predicted that there would be an original parquet wood floor underneath.

"You look really pretty today," he said, and I blushed.

"Stop." I sucked at flirting.

"I've hit a roadblock."

I followed his eyes to the direction of the dining room. Agnes sat in the middle of the room. She held her head tall on her little neck.

Agnes was my cat, a beautiful orange tabby. Who'd taken to talking to me the minute I moved back to my haunted hometown. Given what I'd seen since I'd moved back here, Agnes' ability to communicate with me was one of the more normal occurrences of my day. As Agnes looked at Grady with defiance in her golden eyes, Bubba Smith, my giant Bull Mastiff, and Agnes's slave, dragged a pair of boots into the dining room. He turned around, and from the looks of the debris in the room, he had been depositing stuff all day.

I'd cleared the room of tables, chairs, and boxes so Grady could remove the carpet. It was now filled with cat toys, dog toys, dog beds, my shoes, welcome mats, my recently relocated boots, and just about anything Bubba could carry in his mouth.

"What the heck?" I looked from Agnes to Bubba, to Grady.

"Every time I get one thing cleaned out, to start removing your rug, your dog brings in another."

"I'd think with your, uh, heritage, you'd know how to handle canines."

"I do, and never in my life have I encountered a brother so under the control of a feline." Grady looked at my two room-mates and furrowed his brow.

Agnes responded with her usual attitude, disdain. She sniffed in our general direction.

"We do not want a hardwood floor, and this beast doesn't want to cooperate with us."

"Agnes, I've asked Grady to remove the old carpet. Even you said it was gauche."

"It is, but we do not think hardwood in here is comfortable. Bubba is carrying out my protest to your ill-advised home décor decisions."

"I can see that. Can we compromise?" As I negotiated Bubba dragged a colander from the kitchen into the room.

I took a deep breath. I would never win an argument with Agnes.

"What if I buy that soft bed and scratching post thing you were eyeing on Chewy.com?" Agnes was discriminating.

"I'll need the shag one. And get this mongrel to construct a proper door for Bubba. The current one is too small."

"Deal, I'll get you the fancy bed and have Grady construct a new egress suitable for you two."

"Deal, also you need new kitchen cabinets. None of this flooring looks right with those NASTY old things."

"One major project at a time, okay?" I walked in and grabbed the flotsam that Bubba had littered in the dining room.

Bubba leaned down so Agnes could crawl up on his back. The two made a royal exit.

"Sorry about that. Agnes had some demands."

"Ugh, cats," Grady said. He didn't question the fact that I was just negotiating terms with my house pets. In Widow's Bay, it was run of the mill.

"Sorry." I looked around. Other than the dining room, it appeared the rest of the house was now carpet-free. The wood floors were scuffed and dull, but they were there.

"Wow, you were right about the floors. They're everywhere!"

"A big improvement over that mauve wall to wall."

"It was a thing, mauve, in the eighties. My mom loved it." This house had been in my family for generations. I'd grown up here, it was a gorgeous, historical Victorian, but it was in severe need of an upgrade.

"My guys have time tomorrow, with a little help I can get these refinished fast. They're in pretty good shape."

"Great."

"You eat dinner yet?"

"No, I haven't. I have to go back out, another story to cover."

"Well, you have to eat. Let's go grab a bite." I didn't know if this was a date, if it required a Facebook status change, or if it was just dinner. Or did he actually want to bite me? All were on the table in this town these days I realized.

"You like Mexican?" I asked. I happened to know Esther's Authentic Mexican Cuisine was enough to lead a man to shift into a bear.

"Sure."

"Okay, follow me to Esther's."

"I can drive, bring you back here?"

"No, no trouble." I wanted my own car, my own escape route if need be.

"Afraid I'll get fresh in the truck?"

"I've got enough mind readers in my life. See you at Esther's downtown."

"See you in fifteen minutes, snag a table for three. Meet you there."

Grady was out the door.

"I like the vampire better than this werewolf. The vampire has custom-made shirts."

"As usual I didn't ask your opinion."

CHAPTER 6

I switched my work jeans for a pair of dinner jeans and drove to Esther's. It was right around the corner from my friend Georgie's bookstore and deer processing operation, The Broken Spine, and not too far from the office I just left.

Things were a little quieter than they were during last month's All Souls Fest, but there was a definite uptick in activity in my town. Ski season was in full swing, and the Yule Days festival that Candy and Pauline were planning wasn't too far away.

Esther herself greeted me.

"Hey, Marzie, when are you going to add a restaurant section to Your U.P. News? Highlight Fish Taco Tuesday? Double Marg Thursdays?"

"I'll put that in my editor's suggestion box. With all the tourism it could be pretty useful to do restaurant reviews. Can I get a table for three?"

"Yep, follow me." Esther directed me to a table by the window and left the menus.

"Quesadilla, with cheese, guac, and optional jalapeno on special tonight."

"Thanks."

I watched as Grady and a little boy entered the restaurant.

I wasn't the only one watching. He was all lumberjack plaid and well-worn jeans cool. And there was always a sparkle in his eyes. I had to admit I liked Grady. A lot.

Walking behind him was a towheaded little boy. And there was something very familiar about him.

They got to my table, and I figured it out.

"Hi there, this is my son, Craddock. You've met before, in a way."

"I'm five."

"Well hi, Craddock, have a seat!" I now felt quite ridiculous about the idea I'd had of Grady putting the moves on me at dinner.

"My friends call me Crad."

"Got it, that's a unique name, Crad. Mine's Marzie. Also, kind of different."

"Yes. Can I get nachos?" Crad said to Grady.

"Whatever you want."

I looked closer at Crad and my notion of how I knew him firmed up.

"You're the lady from the woods," Crad said.

"I am." This little boy wasn't a little boy the last two times I'd met him. He was a wolf puppy! A fluffy white wolf puppy.

"You saved me from becoming dinner that night I think."

"I like you!" Crad said, and I smiled. I'd stumbled upon a werewolf funeral ceremony while I was digging around for a story. The wolves involved did not like the intrusion and Crad, in the form of a puppy, put himself in between sharp white teeth and me.

"I owe you dinner at least, and they have chocolate brownies for dessert."

"Dad?"

"Yep, if you have room for all that."

"I will," Crad said with confidence.

I looked at Grady.

"Can I ask you a few questions about, well, how this works?" I flashed my eye at Crad above his blonde head to indicate what I meant.

"Sure, not for the news though, right? Staying out of the papers keeps us alive."

"No, not the news. It's just my Aunt and the older ladies, and even the people who've been here a long time seem to know how the shifting and other things work. I have no idea."

"Fire away."

I started to launch into the list of questions as Crad dumped a packet of sugar on the table.

"Crad!" Grady shook his head.

"I got this." I put a hand out to the little boy.

"Here, come with me."

Crad took my hand, and we walked got up from the table and walked back to the hostess station.

"I just wanted to see if I could make a sugar mountain," Crad said to me as we scooted away from Grady, who was trying to scoop the mess into a napkin.

"Totally get it," I said. We found Esther again.

"You still keep that activity basket for young patrons? The one my boys liked so much?"

"Sure do." Esther produced a basket of coloring books, crayons, and some tabletop games.

"Perfect."

We walked back to the table and I laid the treasures out in front of my new little friend. He dove in with gusto. The sugar packets were now safe, for the time being anyway.

"How did you know they had that?" Grady asked me.

"Mother of twin sons. Entertaining little boys at restaurants is a specialty of mine."

"I'm grateful. How old are your little boys?"

"Not so little, they're in college."

"That's hard to believe, you're so young."

"Right." The flattery was sweet, but over the top.

Our waitress came over.

"Esther said quesadillas are on special. I'll take that."

"Make that two. And keep the tortilla chips coming."

"Do they have mac and cheese?" Little Craddock asked his dad.

"We don't, but we can put a ton of cheese on the tacos," the waitress offered with a smile.

"Okay, thank you, ma'am."

"Craddock, that was really nice manners," I said to the boy, and his smiling face beamed up at me.

There was something so sweet about a Dad and son combo. It almost made me want to have little kids again. Almost.

I returned to the questions I had about, well, everything.

"So, the questions. How are werewolves, uh, made?"

"We're not made, we're born." I looked at Crad, now profoundly engrossed in coloring, even so, I lowered my voice.

"Is Crad's mom a werewolf too?"

"No, my mate was human. Only boys shift by the way. Girls, well that's a story for another day."

"Oh, okay, you said was?"

"Died when Crad was a baby." For the first time, I saw sadness in Grady's normally happy eyes.

"I'm sorry." I moved on quickly. I didn't want to bring up something sensitive, especially in front of the sweet little boy. His blonde locks reminded me of my Sammie, he was golden-haired and sometimes white-haired in the summer. While his brother Joe had my dark wavy hair. They were twins, but no one ever guessed it.

"It was a long time ago. We're looking forward right now, thanks to being here in Widow's Bay."

"Marzie, did you know the bad men were trying to get us,

'cause I turned, and then Dad turned, right in the middle of Meijer's! Disaster!"

Meijer was the Walmart of Michigan, and I could imagine the scene.

"It was near the deli section. I underestimated how pungent the salami was that day." Grady pointed a finger over the boy's head.

"I guess that's my next question. When do you shift, how often?"

"Now that we're here, in Widow's Bay, we can control it. That's why we have to be here. The longer we're away, the worse our ability to master it is."

"I wound up in the dog pound!" Craddock said, and my eyes were as wide as his.

"Oh my."

"Yeah, Dad came and got me."

"I can't even imagine."

"Well, I shifted too, defensively. So then I had to escape out of the store, because, you see, the typical grocery shopper in Battle Creek isn't expecting to stop an alpha wolf running at top speed."

"But they caught me with a net. They had bacon."

"Hard to resist," I said to the sweet little boy.

"You must have been so upset," I said to Grady.

"The gate was opened in the nick of time let's just say. I had to make like I was in the market for adopting a shelter dog to get this pup back home."

"But now you're here. And safe!"

"Just working to be sure there are lumber jobs ready to go. Candy says she's got that pretty well taken care of, especially after she's elected."

"Yeah, if the rumor mill doesn't turn the town against her."

"We have to be sure she does. It will be a lot easier having a friend in office than that Schutte asshole." Grady said.

"Dad, you owe me." Craddock put out his hand, without looking up from his crayon creation.

Grady, in a similar move, never took his eyes from me as he fished into his pocket and deposited a quarter into Crad's cute little palm.

"Candy's key to you staying?" I hadn't considered that.

"No, we're here, and more are on the way. Candy and the rest of you ladies are key to us having productive employment in the logging business. In the case of the vamps, you're key in making sure to keep Brule in the loop on all sorts of stuff. We're all coming now, but it's better if you witches are in charge. Instead of the Schutte Heads of the world."

"Dad!"

"I said Schutte Head. You have a dirty mind, kiddo."

I knew about my role with Brule and had performed the task, even though I hadn't fully embraced the idea that I was The Liaison between the oldest living vampire and the residents of Widow's Bay.

"Ridge Schutte is against every single thing Candy's for, so you're right there."

"And we're going to have enough to deal with fighting off other enemies much less fighting inside Widow's Bay."

"Other enemies?" The words produced a strange dread in my chest.

"Not everyone likes the idea of Yooper Naturals as your Aunt calls us. Hell, we can't even agree in our own community how to co-exist. As long as we've been on this earth, people have fought against us. The last thing we need to deal with right now is blowback from some jerky little crooked politician."

I decided to tackle one mystery at a time and get back to understanding werewolves.

"So, are you shifters? Is that the right word?"

"We're highest on the shifter food chain. Werebears are next, your occasional werecougars, werecoyotes, and then the idiot weremoose."

"Idiot weremoose?"

"If you give a weremoose a muffin!" Craddock chimed in. We all burst out laughing at his play on words.

"The book's not far off though, weremoose are always slowly muddling things up," Grady said and I nodded. Though I had no idea what that might mean.

Our food came, and I had a really lovely time laughing with little Craddock and learning from Grady. I felt like I had a better handle now on the shifters here in Widow's Bay. And how important it was for their survival to be able to control the shifting. I shuddered to think of the sweet little Craddock in a dog pound, alone, afraid, and confused.

The little boy had saved me once, and I owed him as much as I owed his Dad. They were brave, these two.

The conversation was easy with Grady and with Craddock, and before we knew it, the meal was over. Our waitress brought the check. I paid. I didn't want Grady to think, well, dating wasn't in my wheelhouse of skills at this point.

"Wait, you shouldn't be paying for our dinner."

"You can get it next time, and besides, you had to shell out what, seventy-five cents for that language."

"A dollar," Craddock corrected.

"Yikes," Grady said.

"Here!" Craddock presented me with a lovely drawing. "It's the forest by where we live, so you don't get lost again okay?"

"Thank you. It's beautiful and useful. I've got the perfect spot for it on my refrigerator."

"Cool!" Craddock bounded in front of Grady as we made our way out of the restaurant.

"Buckle up," Grady said as the boy climbed into the truck.

"Thanks for letting me pick your brain."

"Craddock is in love with you."

"Ah, well."

"You're good with us, our kind," Grady said, and I felt the blush rise from my neck to my cheeks.

"I'm good with wild little shifters? Who knew?" I teased.

"Especially the wild ones."

"He's charming, and only a little wild. Like all boys should be."

"Next time I think I'm going to leave Craddock with a sitter."

"So you can swear all you like?"

"And other things." I felt my face flush. I wished I could blame a double margarita, except I hadn't had one.

"I'll leave the front door open for you tomorrow. I've got one more stop to make for work tonight, so I'll see you then." I stepped back away from the potentially date-like finish to dinner with Grady.

"Sounds good, boss. I'll get that carpet up now that your cat has given you the okay."

"Sorry, she's really the boss."

"They always are, damn cats." Grady turned to walk to his truck. I headed for my Jeep, which was parked around the corner.

I couldn't help smiling at how nice the night had been. And how easy it was to hang out with Grady and Craddock.

I didn't realize I was being followed until it was too late.

CHAPTER 7

My mind was filled with the events of the day. I wondered about how Earl McGowan wound up in the pond. I reminded myself about checking water levels. And I thought about all I'd learned about shifters. They were born, not made. I wondered about how one parented a little boy who inadvertently shifted into a wolf at the deli counter!

I also thought about Grady. He was fun, funny, and I liked how easy it was to be around him. And then I remembered, he was a werewolf. Not only that. He did have a little boy.

I'd done my time as a mom of little ones. The gap between Pam Ulmer and me wasn't that wide, and it would be easy to find a reason to parent a little boy again.

Which of course was ridiculous since all I'd shared with Grady was the Quesadilla Special. Oh, wow, that sounded dirty. Anyway…

I clicked the door lock on my Jeep. It was only seven o'clock. Early really, and plenty of time to check out the other idea I'd had for a story. I was glad I let Grady know I had other things to do. It helped provide me with a smooth exit; well smooth for me. Which is relative I guess.

The Upper Peninsula Bigfoot/Sasquatch Research Organization held meetings six times a year all over the U.P. This month's last meeting of the year was in Widow's Bay.

The stated aim of UPBSRO was to document and research, not capture or hurt, any bigfoot creature they'd come across. They were about education, not hunting, according to their literature.

Tonight's meeting was being held at the Independent Order of Oddfellows Union Hall. It was a small facility, one that rented out for a modest donation, and so the dozen concerned bigfoot researchers easily filled it up. There was a tray of cold cuts, deviled eggs, various sandwich breads, and a variety of two-liters of pop available for attendees. They enjoyed their food while the head of the organization appeared to be having an existential crisis of epic proportions.

"It's about branding. We're known as the Bigfoot/Sasquatch Research Organization. It is on our jackets. Our beer koozies. And the Facebook!" Ray Tandler, president and founder, was passionate about the subject at hand. And holding on to calm by the thinnest of threads.

"Look, Ray, it's not a bigfoot, it's probably one of the shifters. That's an observable fact," Russell Nopper chimed in, trying to calm Ray down. I recognized most of the assembled members at the meeting. Though some faces were strangers, probably out-of-towners in for the undoubtedly pivotal discussion over the future of the organization.

"So what do we do about the beer koozies I've got in bulk in my basement?" Ray went on. Behind him there was a split screen of what I supposed was a Sasquatch sighting from the 1970s maybe. Next to it was a picture of a sighting that I'd missed witnessing in person, by a few seconds. I couldn't verify that the first picture was real. But I knew, without a doubt, that the second one was an accurate account of what happened in downtown Widow's Bay.

A very nice and good-looking man had been walking down Main when Esther's fish taco special sparked him to shift into a bear in broad daylight.

It had caused Pauline to crash her car and sent Georgie in search of something for the beefy bear man to wear. Seeing as the shifting had rendered him butt naked.

I should have known someone would have gotten a picture of that event with their cell phones. The fact that it wasn't plastered on the nightly news had to be because, typically, only a handful of people really believed Ray's claims on most things. I realized now that Ray was right, not bent.

"I alerted the media with this picture, and it was the same as usual, no one cared." It was just as I suspected.

"But look here, though, sneaking in the back row, the media." Damn, Ray had seen me come in, and now everyone turned around in their metal folding chairs to look at me.

"Hi, well, see I did pay attention. Saw you were having a meeting. I got your news release about it." I tried to sink into a chair and make myself invisible. It wasn't working.

"You're from the rinky-dink UP Your News, lotta good that's going to do. We have major developments. TMZ should be here," Ray said. The disappointment that I wasn't the network or TMZ was palpable.

"Your U.P. News," I corrected him.

"What do you think, Marzie, should we change our name, now that we have this picture of a bear man?" Russell asked me.

"I'm not supposed to influence events you know, I'm supposed to cover them. You need to do what's best for the UPBSOR."

"UPBSRO," Ray corrected me.

"Marzie, cut the crap. You solved the Lottie Bradbury murder. How was that not influencing events?" Chet, a neighbor of Lottie's, chimed in. I was surprised to see Chet here, though why I was surprised at anything anymore was a mystery. And he made a valid point. Lottie's murder might have gone unsolved if I hadn't noticed a few things Loof and his crew missed.

"Fine. What names are on the table?"

"I like the Upper Peninsula Bear Man Research Organization," Chet said.

"Just cause's there's evidence of a bear man doesn't mean there's not a Sasquatch," Ray pointed out.

"Honestly, Ray has a point," I said, and there was a lot of nodding. Chet rolled his eyes at me.

"You agree we should keep the name?"

My mind raced to the fact that they were trying to get national attention for their photo. I studied it. Objectively, as if I didn't know it was real. Honestly, it wasn't much better than the old seventies photo. The figure was dark, hairy, and walking on four legs. Quality wise, the bear man picture was almost as blurry as the old Sasquatch snapshot.

"Do you have proof of the shifter part? I mean, that looks like a photo of something bear-ish."

"No, just the bear, it shifted before anyone realized what was happening, then disappeared."

"So, if you change your name, does that mean you admit that all Bigfoot slash Sasquatch encounters were bears?"

"Heck no! See what I'm saying?" Ray looked to his membership to bolster his position.

"She's got a point," Russell conceded.

"Fine fine, motion to change the name rescinded," Chet said, and Ray shot me a look of gratitude. I responded with a weak smile. I had no idea what I was going to write about if this was the only order of business. If I turned in a story about verified bear shifter sightings, I'd be out of a job. It was hard enough for me to believe it and I'd seen it with my own eyes.

Luckily, they moved on to other business.

"Tom, where are we on the slideshow to the senior centers?" A member I didn't know stood up to answer.

"All done, if approved tonight we can roll it out to communities throughout the U.P."

They shared the slideshow on Bigfoot/Sasquatch awareness and education. I soaked it in. That would be my report, the effort at outreach in the upper part of the state. Yes. Phew. I could garner plenty of material for a little story that didn't include the debate over bear shifters.

It was a relief.

As I left, Ray even handed me a beer koozie.

"Thanks, Marzie, you know and I know there's a lot out there."

"Sure. The story will be online tomorrow. And we'll link to your senior center tour calendar too."

The meeting wrapped up, and I headed out. It was late now. And I resisted the innate urge to hustle home.

I realized that on a night like this if I were a young mom, I'd have to hurry and apologize to everyone and their brother about why I was late. I would have to feel guilty for missing dinner, or bedtime, or whatever.

Ha! Empty Nesting was the new twenties! I thought as I drove home. I hoped the Distinguished Ladies could convince poor Pam of that perspective so her teenage boy could get to college without another episode where he was trapped in a baby's body, and a onesie. The thought played in my mind as I rolled forward on the pitch-dark road home.

I didn't see it, but something made a loud thump and rocked the Jeep.

I slammed on my brakes and looked in the rearview. Had I hit something?

My heart pounded. Had I been too immersed in my thoughts that I'd stopped paying attention to where I was driving?

It was dark, and the road was deserted. Maybe I'd hit a pothole?

I put the car in park. I needed to see what I'd done. There was no doubt something hit my Jeep. I stepped out into the cold air. My breath was visible, but not much else was. There were no street lights, or other cars. It was a kind of dark that you didn't get in the city or even the suburbs. My heart was still beating fast after the bump in the night. I shook it off. I wasn't a timid person by nature. I needed to see if I hit something and stop getting spooked by the dark.

I walked around to the back of my Wrangler. There was nothing there.

I focused my attention into the tree line at the side of the road. Maybe what I hit went flying?

Still nothing. I walked around the Jeep to the passenger side.

And there it was. A dent. Nothing huge, but I knew my Wrangler like the back of my hand, and this dent was new.

Had something crashed into the front end somehow while I was driving?

Where was it now?

I was alone on the road. There wasn't another car or a wounded animal in sight. People had actually died hitting deer out here. I'd read the story on the news before, over 50,000 deer vs. car crashes happened in the state every year.

The night was quiet. Surely if I'd hit a deer, I'd hear it now? If it was still alive.

Whatever made that dent was gone.

I walked back to the front of my Jeep.

Before I could climb in, I was flung away from it. I was swept up.

It was disorienting, and so fast I had a hard time processing how I'd gone from standing to constrained in the blink of an eye.

"What the hell?" A man held me around my waist.

Well, he was man-shaped.

If I had any doubt what a blood-sucking vampire looked like when he or it was about to suck blood, it was gone in this instant.

"HEY! Let me go!" I squirmed, I put my hands on his chest,

and I quickly realized I was trapped. The vampire's skin was white, his hair was shiny and dark. His eyes were red and focused on my neck, not on my screaming.

Unlike Brule's old world-ish, European flair, this one wore modern clothes, a North Face jacket, actually and jeans. He looked like he would fit in on campus with my sons. A vampire wearing a North Face, something about that was hilarious, I was just too concerned about being drained of my blood to put my finger on what in that instant. Did vampires feel the cold? Was it a fashion statement?

"This won't take long," he said to me.

"What won't take long? Killing me?" He bared white teeth at me.

I screamed. It felt like a futile waste of my remaining breath, but I had no other play.

He leaned over me, and I felt a pinch on my neck. It reminded me of a bee sting, maybe that's all it would be? I could handle that.

I felt my body relax. Was the bee sting a venom to immobilize the prey?

I thought, with regret, that I should have interrogated Brule or Dorothy in the same way I'd done to Grady earlier. Maybe then I'd know. Vampire illiteracy was about to prove deadly in my case.

I was falling. At first it was falling into some sort of trance or something, and then it was actual falling onto the ground on the side of the road. The snow was cold on my back. And it woke me up from whatever trance the initial skin prick had caused.

Brule, was there, with an arm around the North Face vampire's throat.

"Cease."

My attacker struggled a second. But Brule was bigger, stronger, and I'd guess hundreds of years older. He forced the North Face Vampire to his knees.

"We don't feed in Widow's Bay," he said to the younger vampire.

The red eyes turned brown. His fangs disappeared.

"Bro, I was just so hungry, like munchies hungry."

"No one taught you this?" Brule asked the North Face vampire.

"Uh, no."

"Typical."

"Head south, to the Casino. There are truckers, travelers, and gamblers there that you can snack on." The North Face vampire nodded, and Brule let him go. He looked at me one more time, in the same way I look at bagel with cream cheese after a week of low carb dieting.

"Come back to me afterward. We will instruct you." The North Face vampire disappeared as fast as he appeared. Brule issued the order as though there was no doubt the North Face vampire would have to follow it.

Brule rushed to my side and helped me up. He looked at my neck, which felt intact. Though for all I knew my thyroid gland could be rolling toward the roadside ditch. I was still feeling the effects of the prick from the North Face Vampire, I guessed.

"Ma chère."

"French? Really?"

"I'll drive you home." I wanted to protest. I was ready to lock and load my independent woman speech, except my independent woman legs buckled underneath me.

"Yeah, probably a good idea." Brule swept me up in his arms and deposited me in the front of my Jeep. He got behind the wheel.

"Your oil light is on. I'd get that checked, chère."

"Right."

"Never get out of your vehicle in the night."

"I thought I hit a deer or a person or something."

"It was a crude trick of that young one, but it worked."

"Yep, sure did. What were you saying, vampires are not allowed to eat us here, in Widow's Bay?"

"We don't eat flesh, we aren't Zombies for heaven's sake."

"Okay, so drink blood in town, pardon my ignorance."

"Well we can, but it would be quite rude."

"Quite."

I flipped down the mirror on my visor to get a look at my neck. I couldn't see any damage, though I did see a little red spot. It looked more like a mosquito bite of the damned than anything life-threatening. I had Brule to thank for that, I was sure.

"I will discover who made him, and he will be punished."

"What?"

"Whoever made him let him out without supervision or education. That is irresponsible and puts us all at risk."

"So there's an onboarding?"

"Explain onboarding."

"You know when you get hired at a company and HR gives you the benefits info, the logins to the computer, directions to the breakroom, corporate culture mission statement and what not."

I was making a joke, sort of, it was my way to cope with the utter terror I'd just experienced. Brule, as usual, looked at me like I was speaking in tongues when I tried to be funny.

"I do not know this term, ayechar. No matter, we must not make new, young ones if we do not have the desire to mentor them for a time, a year preferably."

As we drove to my house, my curiosity pushed aside my terror at nearly getting sucked dry. I'd gotten the scoop on were-wolves 101, and now I needed to add to my Yooper Natural knowledge base with vampires. It appeared my life depended on it.

"So, shifters are born not made, but vampires?"

"Made not born."

"Gotcha. And are all the rules true?"

"Rules, you mean mirrors and crucifixes?"

"Yeah, or garlic."

"I can be seen in a mirror, and rather like it."

"Rightly so, you're a silver fox." I decided it was fun to drop current references into conversations with Stephen AKA Etienne Brule. It was the only time I had the slightest bit of the upper hand.

"No, I'm not able to shift into a fox."

"Silver fox, good-looking gray-haired dude."

"Oh, I see. Is a dude the same as a bro?" A smile played at the corners of his mouth.

"Yeah, pretty much, so go on with the rules please?"

"Garlic is fine, crucifixes are fine, religious iconography isn't harmful to us unless we think it is. That young one might have seen a movie and decided he should recoil from a cross but if he had any education from his maker whatsoever he'd know that was false."

"You're impervious to just about anything."

"Daylight reduces us to cinders and ash."

"That could so be the name of a rock band. Ha! Uh, good to know, no sparkling vamps before twilight."

"Correct, we incinerate rather quickly."

"Ouch."

"Also why I need you, chère, as my Liaison."

"Yeah, Liaison, I think I need onboarding for that."

"I'm attempting it right now, pay attention love. We must go to ground here in Widow's Bay and in a few other places. I was made here. So were many of the progeny. There are a few places in the world like Widow's Bay. And we may stay away for decades, but eventually, we need this earth, or we begin to corrupt."

"Corrupt? That sounds bad. Just like the shifters."

"It is bad, we're here now so hopefully the danger is past on that issue."

"So you make vampires how?"

"Drain and then fill. That one the movies got right."

"And about blood? Can you suck on a squirrel in a pinch?"

"Human, accept no substitutes. Though you can get some from a blood bank. We have special ones for the pacifists among us."

"Yikes."

"Young ones are taught not to feed where you sleep."

"Smart business plan."

"I am deeply sorry you've been attacked. It is incredibly rude."

"And flipping traumatizing. You act like that North Face wearing dude used the wrong fork at dinner."

"Yes, traumatizing for certain." Brule looked stung by my reaction, and I felt immediately sorry that I'd been flippant.

"We are here." Brule pulled into the driveway of my home. "I will see you to your doorstep."

"That's not needed."

"Your safety is important to Widow's Bay, and to me." It seemed like he wasn't talking about the gig as a Liaison all of a sudden.

I opened my door and got out. Nothing like a little evasion to avoid the man's intense stare. Was date dodging a sport? Because I was becoming a pro.

I expected Brule to follow me to the back door, but instead, he was drawn to my big front porch. The Victorian design of the home had features you couldn't find in today's McMansions, and the large wraparound front porch was one.

"Many memories here," Brule said into the night air, not really to me.

I wondered how he kept them all in his brain.

"How old are you, or is that rude to ask?"

"I was born in '92 as a human. And I was made, as a vampire, in 1640."

"Holy, uh, wow. I can't really believe it. I'm having a hard time with all of the mystical, uh. I don't know." He meant 1592. Holy mackeral.

"This land, I brought your ancestors to it in the 1690s." Based on what Georgie had found and The Crones had alleged, the ancestors were the Witches of Salem. He had saved them, some of them anyway. Unpacking this information always caused me to fear the responsibility these concepts carried. There was a legacy that I was supposed to be carrying on, it was a weight that I tried to carry lightly and failed. When confronted with the mystical my mind grabbed for something normal, something plain.

My panic was visible and more pronounced than when I thought I was about to be a roadside snack. I struggled to come to terms with the age of this man on my porch and the ancient nature of my town.

Brule stepped forward and leaned his head down to within an inch of mine. Our eyes locked. I always felt he saw me, but also beyond me. Did I look like the witches who came before me? Did I sound like them? Were my powers weaker or stronger? I would bet weaker, seeing as I still didn't know how to cast a proper spell.

Brule put his hand behind my head, at the base of my neck. I reached up and used his muscular arm to steady myself. He gently touched his forehead to mine. I felt calmer, I felt steady, and I felt, for a second, that I was up to the task. Whatever that may be. But then, something shifted.

In a whoosh, the porch was gone. In front of my eyes was an image of a woman. She wore tattered clothes. She looked afraid and I saw as she clasped a strong hand. I knew it was his, Brule's. He enfolded her in his arms and I felt her relief.

Then the scene changed again. A man with a cross around his neck closed in on a log cabin. There were others behind him, with fire. They were murderous looking.

I saw the same women, but this time she wasn't afraid, the

word for her in this vision was fierce. Her dark hair was parted at the center and now had a streak of white, like mine. She linked hands with other women, women who looked familiar, but I couldn't name. A torrent of rain came down on the men with the torches.

I knew as sure as I knew my own name that the women he'd showed me had joined forces to save Brule, that he was inside that cabin. The men with torches aimed to destroy him with fire.

I didn't know the timeframe he'd shown me. Was this a great-grandmother I'd seen? Were they Georgie, Fawn, Pauline, Candy and Tatum's ancestors too? Brule didn't answer my fevered thoughts, except he nodded. As if I was right, I had understood what he meant to show me.

"I need to sit down." I hadn't really asked before, whether what I'd heard from Georgie's research was true. Brule had shared his memories with me now. He was giving me that proof. Georgie's documents and Aunt Dorothy's stories were real. They were my history and the history of this coven I'd found myself a part of.

Brule guided me to the old porch swing. I plopped down, and he sat next to me. His eyes were softer now, with concern. He should be concerned. This stuff was bananas.

"You understood what you saw?"

"Those were your memories?"

"And your ancestor's too."

"You helped her escape the hangings at Salem."

"Yes, and her friends, her sisters. There are others here, that I found later, they had nothing to do with Salem. There were those outcast from the tribes here, persecuted just the same."

"Wow."

"But then you saw them do the same for me. Escape the torches. What is the phrase you use now, ah, yes, it is a two-way street?"

I smiled, he had made a joke, sort of.

"They clasped hands. They were using the same sort of power I have with my friends."

"Yes, but as powerful and brave as Sarah was, as they all were, you have more raw talent. You are just uncertain, new."

"That's putting it mildly. Her name was Sarah Nurse?"

"Yes, Rebecca Nurse died, was hanged. But I was able to save her daughter. You have her soul, her intelligence, her strength, but more."

"What if I can't... what if I don't? If I mess up, people or Yoopers could get hurt."

"You will, uh, mess up. Every creature does."

"Reassuring."

Brule leaned in again, and this time our lips connected. It was a soft kiss. It was imbued with nothing but the current moment. It was sweet, but I also couldn't forget it was dangerous. This person, or vampire, just told me blood was how he survived.

I best not forget any of it.

"I'm tired. Thank you for swooping in and explaining some of this, uh craziness of Widow's Bay."

"Yes, onboarding for The Liaison."

"I guess we both learned a thing or two tonight."

"No more leaving your vehicle. No matter what you hit."

"Yes."

I walked to the door and opened it. Brule stood for a moment as I crossed my threshold. I turned to look at him. His white hair glowed now in the moonlight. He watched me intensely. Did he want to come in?

I closed the door.

That was enough onboarding for one night.

CHAPTER 8

"No water in the lungs," I looked at the report Loof handed me. The initial exam was in on Earl McGowan.

"Right," Loof said as I handed it back to him.

"So he didn't drown." Reading an autopsy report was a skill I had acquired over years of reporting on murders in Detroit for WXYD.

"Nope, and it looks like he was dead before he hit the water. No signs of bruising either. We expected seatbelt marks or something. But nothing."

"So?"

"Sheriff Budd's signing off on this. We're officially ruling it suspicious."

"Do you think he was murdered? Gut reaction now."

"Yep, I think he was murdered."

"Any suspects?"

"No. None at this time. His daughter-in-law, your friend Tatum, says the family is estranged from him, but officially, nothing official. We're interviewing people who last saw him."

"Who would that be?"

"Can't say, part of the investigation." Loof's desk phone rang.

"Yep, headed in right now," Loof hung up his phone and stood up. "Gotta go Marzie, roll call."

"Sure, thanks Loof."

"Oh, and that fluff recipe thing you gave Mary Jo, excellent! Forgot to tell ya that. She made some for the office." I smiled, and he headed toward his roll call meeting.

I did a quick look around. No one was paying any attention to me. I stood up and hovered my phone over the piece of paper Loof had been eyeing. I snapped a quick picture.

It wouldn't be in the story, whatever I found, but it would at least give me a heads up on what to follow up on in the possible murder of Earl McGowan.

I looked around. No one saw my little covert operation, so I left with a little more than I came in with and a little more than what the police wanted to share. Which is a mark of a good investigative reporter in my opinion.

While I was in The Barrel, I decided to pay Candy a visit. Offices of the City of Widow's Bay were also here.

Candy had a city council office, for now. Eventually, she'd get that top floor office. I was sure of it.

"People loved you ladies in the parade for All Souls, can you whip up something like that for the Yule Days?"

I poked my head around the door and in the chairs facing Candy, as she paced behind her desk, were none other than the remaining three members of the DLC, Dorothy, Frances, and Maxine.

"Only if it's authentic. We're not circus performers," Maxine said. Candy saw me and waved me in.

"Hi, yes, of course, only if it's authentic," Candy said, and the ladies all acknowledged my entrance.

"What are you working on?" I asked.

"We're trying to plan what the ladies are going to do for Yule Days. We need that Celtic witch vibe again," Candy explained.

"Oh, isn't it so sweet that people like it." Aunt Dorothy said to her friends.

"Tourists sure do," Candy added.

"What's on the table, and can I report that you're all working to plan the festival? Could be a nice little article on Your U.P. News?"

"Heck yes, I need some positive press," Candy said. I was already glad I stopped in. I was still driven by the need to show the Your U.P. News people that this former anchorwoman had news chops to spare.

"It's all about Yule, mulled wine, and I could dance naked." I looked at Frances, and she was totally serious.

"I don't think that will be necessary. The tourists coming in include families," Candy cautioned.

"They can dance naked too." Frances didn't see the issue.

"Let's put a pin in that idea for now." Candy said to Frances and then shot a look at me that clearly telegraphed the phrase help!

"Dear Frances, remember, the kids today are very uptight," Aunt Dorothy said to her lifelong friend, and I wondered just what they'd all gotten up to back in their day. Maybe I didn't want to know.

"Brule and his lot, they need to be in on the planning. They'll pack in the tourists." Maxine chimed in.

"They won't be too scary?" Candy said.

"No, they're all handsome, strong, mysterious, and if I were looking for a girls' weekend, and didn't live here already, visiting a place where I might get randy with a shifter or a vampire would be tops on my list!"

"Aunt Dorothy!"

"She's right though." Candy put the kibosh on my puritanical outrage. I squeezed my eyes shut trying to expunge the thought of Aunt Dorothy getting "randy," whatever that was in her parlance.

"It is the winter holiday. I'd use that new resort. Brule's staff can help you, I'm certain." Aunt Dorothy, at her heart, knew how to organize. She was a problem solver. The line between Aunt Dorothy's brand of mayoral moxie and Candy's was straight. It was easy to see how my Aunt had run this town in her day. And I had to say I was happy that Candy was tapping into the experience and knowledge of the Distinguished Ladies, even though one suggested activity included some sort of geriatric Maypole dancing.

"You're right, Dorothy, I'll get with Brule's people at the resort, make sure they're on top of the concepts we're looking at. Thank you all for coming. I appreciate your insights. Just run whatever you're planning by me. Okay? So I can get you the proper venue."

The ladies agreed. They got up and made their goodbyes to Candy and me.

As they walked away, I heard Frances and Maxine, "Oh I read about that Burning Man thing the desert, maybe we could play on that idea, a Melting Man," Frances said to Maxine.

"It's Michigan in December, nothing's melting here," Maxine told her.

"Melting Man, did you hear that, isn't half bad?" I said to Candy.

"Oh, they're good, I just have to walk the line between mystical tourist attraction here and debauchery. Debauchery broker won't look good on my campaign ads."

"That's still on for tonight? The spell or whatever?"

"Damn straight."

"How do you balance this? I mean, practical management of government and well, the ladies, the shifters, and your main developer, Count Dracula of The Fresh Powder?" I was referring of course to Brule, the owner of Samhain Slopes.

Candy put down the paper that she was studying and looked at me with her ice blue eyes. They were a lot like Brule's. A blonde blue-eyed woman, holding Sarah Nurse's hand, flashed in my mind for a second.

"Marzie, you were always searching for something else, somewhere else. I've always known Widow's Bay is the perfect place, because of its eccentricities, not despite them."

The words stung, because they were true, at least a little. I felt bad that I didn't see it when I was younger, or more accurately did see it, and ran away.

"But the magical stuff, that seems to be getting out of control? How do you handle all that in your head? You're a practical person who gets stuff done. I mean… bear shifters?"

"Do that Liaison thing you're supposed to do, that's how we handle the out of control part, and bear shifters, or whatever. We bring a little order to the chaos. Honestly, it all seems like a great way to bring in new tourism money." Candy's eyes lit up a little.

"Really?"

"The mountain, the cold, the Celtic mystery, the Yooper Naturals, no getting rid of it, so let's turn into an asset. Ugh, I'm late for my next meeting."

"Got it, thank you for the perspective. See you tonight. We're doing it at Frog Toe, right?"

"Yep."

I left Candy to her work on behalf of the citizens, human and otherwise, of Widow's Bay.

Her perspective helped me a lot, though I didn't tell her that I nearly became vampire food last night. That wasn't something you put on the brochure. *Skiing! Craft Brews! Celtic Festivals! Undead Attacks! Naked Witches! Visit Widow's Bay Today!* Or maybe you did, what did I know about tourism? I was getting better at accepting the wacky world I was a part of, but still, every day there was some new component to process.

Onward to the day's stories.

I'd write an update on the Yule Days planning meeting, I'd let the world know that the Upper Peninsula Bigfoot/Sasquatch

Research Society had scheduled several new informational sessions as far west as Ontonagon, and free koozies would be distributed to attendees.

Then there was the Earl McGowan update.

That was the tough one. What did we know? Earl was dead before he hit the water. Earl was a bad grandpa.

I wanted more for my follow up story. I looked at my phone, and the snapshot of the notebook Loof had left on his desk.

Loof had written a note that Earl McGowan was last seen two weeks ago at Korda's Hardware and General Store. That was it. That was not much to go on.

Good grief. Was that really all Loof had so far? Earl McGowan went to the hardware store?

I decided it was time for me to pay a visit to Korda's. Maybe I'd find someone to interview, it was worth a try. Plus, Grady said I needed to pick out paint for my dining room anyway. I'd kill two birds with one stone that way.

Korda's was locally owned and operated. I was used to the home improvement megastore in my Detroit suburb. Korda's was the opposite.

At Korda's you could find everything from paint to nails, to penny candy, to bow hunting gear, to raw honey and brown eggs.

I wasn't a DIYer. I never had the time. The twins, the job, and the care and non-feeding of a news anchor had kept me too busy to decoupage or repurpose furniture. But, now, even with getting my bearings in Widow's Bay I'd come to discover I liked spending time redoing my old Victorian home.

Korda's store hadn't changed much over the decades. There was a long wooden counter that ran nearly the length of the space that had been saved from an earlier incarnation. They also kept a potbelly stove with a few chairs where the local old men could chew tobacco, shoot the breeze, and convey to all who entered their expertise in just about everything.

Farming wasn't big in this neck of the woods, but raising livestock was. Owning chickens, cows, and even buffalo wasn't unheard of in rural Widow's Bay. For that you needed feed, so the hardware store also doubled as a feed store.

Three old guys were sitting around the pot belly when I entered. They were all friends with the old owner I supposed. I recognized one as Earl's neighbor, Bertrand Lasko. He seemed to be over the initial grief at losing his neighbor.

"Hello, gentleman. Mind if I sit?" There were four chairs around the stove, and one was conveniently empty.

"Mind? Pretty girl like you can sit where ever you want. Though you should smile more." Oh boy, here we go.

"It's been a while since I was a girl," I said and sat down. I smiled, too. I needed to fit in, not fight, with the geezers.

"She's from the newspaper, be careful what you say." Bertrand Lasko did remember me from our brief encounter. He winked at me as he warned his buddies to clam up.

"There's no such thing as newspapers Bertie, you old fool." The first gentleman chastised Lasko.

"I don't know about that, but Your U.P. News is an online newspaper," I explained.

"Heh heh, Up Your News, that just tickles my boxers," another of the men said. I had the feeling I'd dropped into the Muppet Show skybox.

"I'm doing a follow up on Earl McGowan."

"What, old man dies is about as interesting as dog bites man. No wonder there aren't any newspapers anymore." The first old man was apparently the comedian of the bunch. Lasko nodded in agreement.

"Turns out Earl was dead before he hit the water. The police are calling it suspicious, trying to find out if Earl had enemies."

"He was my best friend. I still can't get over it." Lasko chimed in.

"What? You hated him, we all did. He was mean as a snake and just as warm," the comedian of the group explained.

"That's the rudest thing you've ever said, Arnie. Take it back." Bertie Lasko was on the defense for his neighbor. It was sweet really, though I wondered why his friends didn't believe it.

"You're just mad because he wouldn't sell you his farm, Bertie," Arnie said, I looked at Bertrand Lasko a little more closely.

"Nonsense. No one wants that rock pile," Lasko said, and he nodded to me like it was common knowledge.

"You were trying to buy his farm?" I trained my focus on Lasko.

"Once, a long time ago. I got over that idea."

"How much was it worth?" I asked.

"That is none of the online news' business, as far as I can see." Lasko snapped back and then quickly replaced that with a smile.

"Don't be rude Bertie, this little thing's just doing her job," Arnie came to my defense. It was sort of cute that he thought I needed it.

"Leave us to our mourning young lady. No need to be such a busybody," Bernie said.

"So, can you give me a few quotes about Earl at least? How he was a good friend or something?"

"He was a real jerk," Arnie said. The other two men laughed, Bernie did not.

"Stop, he was a saint, a great friend, and farmer. Now move along," Lasko said.

"Maybe you can find a good quote over at Maggie's Diner. He liked their Denver Omelets," Arnie offered me a bone.

"Really?"

"Who knows. I did see him having lunch about two weeks ago, day after he was in here, with that guy who used to have the car lot on his front yard, Lars, what's that guy's name?" I smiled at Arnie, he was sweet and trying to help.

"Wait, the same one who tried to sell us insurance, and then what, oh yeah Amway? Yeah, Keith Foley, that's his name. Karen Foley, rest her soul, was his mama." Lars, Old Man Number Three, who hadn't spoken up yet, puzzled out who Earl had been eating with.

"That one should be in the news. Earl wasn't the type to eat with anyone, or oh, how do I say this, pay a plug nickel for a sandwich, so it did strike me as odd." Arnie said, and Lasko smacked him on the shoulder to shut him up.

"Thank you, and does Keith Foley live in Widow's Bay?"

"Yeah, though I'm not sure where he works right now. Bounces around, sales guys always do you know," Arnie said.

"You saw him eat lunch with Keith Foley, anything else you'd like to tell me about Earl? Something nice for a follow-up piece I'm working on?" I asked the men. They all took a second to think.

"He kept to himself. That was a gift to the entire town. And we thank him," Arnie said, and Lars laughed, though the laugh morphed into a hacking cough. Bertrand Lasko's mouth was drawn tight into a small wrinkled line.

"Got it, thanks for the info on his lunch date. At least we know he was alive and eating lunch in the last few weeks."

"Yeah, true, and it's actually lucky they found him. No one would have complained that he's missing and usually that pond is way higher. I'd ask about that." Lars added his expertise to the discussion.

"Agree, I'm working on that angle too."

"Yeah, that's the story you should be doing missy, water levels out my way are way more important than Earl McGowan alive or dead," Bertrand Lasko mansplained to me how to do my job. It was delightful.

"Will do. You gentleman have a nice rest of your day."

"Chair's always open, honey." Arnie wagged his eyebrows up and down. I suppressed a laugh. I didn't want to encourage the rampant old guy sexism. But they were funny, well, two of the three of them were funny. Bertrand was not funny, not friendly, and hard to read.

But old guys, sometimes, knew more than the town gossips. They weren't a bad group to have in my wheelhouse for information on what was happening in town.

"Thanks, got some paint to pick out now."

"Avoid the peach hues, not good for brunettes," Lars said, and I nodded. What a trip these three were.

There was a wall of paint samples, and in about one minute I had about five-thousand, give or take, small paper squares in my bag. I was certain Agnes would be the final decision maker on what color looked best with her hair, not mine.

I ended my work day in my actual office.

By the end of business, I'd filed a story on the suspicious death ruling of Earl McGowan, a calendar of events for Sasquatch continuing education classes, and the latest on the Yule Days planning, sans the offer that the Distinguished Ladies dance nude for tourists.

By far the most significant loose end was Earl McGowan. He died suspiciously. He owned valuable land, even though he could barely farm a turnip out of it. Bertrand Lasko, and maybe others, wanted it, though Lasko said that was a long time ago.

The good news was that visiting the hardware store had given me an additional lead: Earl McGowan had lunch with a man named Keith Foley in the last few weeks. That was something. I was going to check on that one tomorrow. Maybe Keith Foley had some ideas or at least a new direction for me.

Tomorrow I would also take a ride out to Earl's farm again and look around. If the suspicious death angle didn't yield follow up stories for me to cover, maybe the water story would.

I FILED my stories and locked up.

It was time to cast a spell.

CHAPTER 9

I showed up at the Frog Toe a little early to be sure Tatum knew the latest on the death of her father-in-law.

She was behind the bar trying to lift a heavy tray of glasses onto a shelf. I watched. She could probably have easily managed the task, but out of nowhere, it seemed, a man with scruffy dark hair, clad in leather pants, a black Judas Priest t-shirt, and with tattoos up and down his arm was at her side. He smoothly grabbed the heavy load she tried to hoist and easily placed it on the shelf. Tatum did not appreciate the assist.

"I told you to watch the door. Chucky Puckett and his brothers are going to try to sneak in, and they're on the white-board," she barked the information to the leather-clad dude, and he gave her a smoldering look. He also did exactly as she said and headed to the door to block the Pucketts, if indeed, they showed up.

"'Thank you' might have also been a good thing to say to the nice leather pants-wearing man who lifts heavy things," I said as I hopped on a stool.

"I can't encourage him. Plus, the Pucketts started a fight over who gets the far corner of the bar. Like they own it. Chucky dumped a beer on one of those loggers who was sitting there minding his own business. The Pucketts still keep trying to slip in when it gets busy. They owe me a dozen new mugs and at least two weeks to cool down before I let them in again."

"And your handy helper there? New bouncer?"

"Yeah, the Yooper Natural that your Brule sent over. Good bouncer but he hovers. I can lift my own damn glasses. Yesterday he punched a guy who slapped my ass." I nodded and wondered if Tatum protested just a bit too much about having a hot as heck new bouncer defending her honor.

"Seems fair, if someone slapped your ass."

"I punch whoever slaps my ass. It's not 1950."

"Right."

"And I'm slightly concerned he might bite me." Tatum filled six frosty mugs as she added the biting concern to her list of reasons not to like her sexy bouncer.

"No worries there, I don't think. Brule says that's a rule, they don't eat where they sleep."

"Makes sense." Tatum waved a waitress over who took the tray of beer.

"Table ten," she said, and the waitress was off.

"You're a little early, what can I get you?"

"Water. I want a clear head for my incantation."

"Good idea." She slid a glass my way.

"So, I've got an update on Earl."

"Still dead?"

"Yes, but suspiciously so."

I let her know what Loof told me about the non-drowning.

"Also, no bruising, even from the seatbelt. That's odd because usually when the belt tightens, you know, when you brake, the body lurches forward, and there's some sign of it, especially after an accident."

"Honey, what's odd is that he had a seatbelt on at all."

"Why?"

"Way back, when Zach was still a toddler, Earl picked him up from kindergarten or something, he pulls into our driveway, and Pat noticed Zach was in the front seat, goes in there to yell at his dad, and realizes not only was he in the front seat, but also no seatbelt."

"Great."

"Yeah, Earl disabled the dinger on all his cars. He thought seatbelts could kill, and cigarettes strengthened the lungs."

"Nice, but that seatbelt thing could be important maybe."

"Cool. Okay, take your water over to the cauldron. I've saved all our seats and Franklin is going to cover. The coven's on the way." Tatum flashed me an evil smile. I rolled my eyes. Coven. We were a coven? I guess we were. Franklin was Tatum's most trusted manager. If he was on board to watch the floor, she'd be able to focus. This was getting real.

In short order Fawn and Georgie arrived, followed by Candy and Pauline. With Tatum and me that made six, twice the number needed to pull together badass magical thingamajigs. This was of course according to Dorothy and confirmed by Georgie's research.

We'd also learned that each one of us brought something unique to the table or cauldron. And that was the true power we were harnessing, our unique gifts in combination with a shared will. This was our first official attempt to put our power into action. Well, it was my first official anyway, the rest had dabbled in helping the kids' opponents botch field goal attempts and bring fog down on a tough team. Dorothy was not pleased about those antics.

Georgie had worked with Dorothy and had assigned us our jobs. Which was part of Georgie's job. She researched what elements were needed, what type of spell would work, and checked the history of Widow's Bay to see if there was already a precedent for our current mission to discover who was sabotaging Candy Hitchcock.

Tatum tended the cauldron, somehow, whether it was craft brew or the craft, she knew what to do. She knew how hot, how long, and precisely when each element needed to be added for the desired effect.

Fawn's job was all physical. She brought herbs, the eye of newt, or hair of political operative, depending on the particular spell.

Pauline and Candy's contributions were less tangible but probably the most important, Dorothy had told Georgie. We weren't entirely sure, but we thought Pauline provided the desire. Her sincere enthusiasm for whatever she did, whether it was Zumba or real estate, translated into something magical around the cauldron. If any one of us, me at the top of the list, was ambivalent about whether the spell would work, Pauline's zeal was the magical counterbalance.

Candy's function was the same in city government or PTA or in spell casting. She served to organize our fragmented focus into a single, compelling goal. This time our goal was to find a rat.

My job was the words, I had to find the words. We all had powers, abilities, and something unique to offer, and these things were continuing to emerge in all of us almost every day. But to do a spell there had to be words that tied everything together. Those words were my job.

I hoped I'd chosen the right ones for tonight's task.

Tatum had her waitress serve us.

"Thanks." Georgie took a sip. Her voice was hoarse.

"You sick?" I asked, and she did look a little flushed.

"Deer gun season nearly kills me every year." The Broken Spine was a bookstore most of the time and a deer processing station during hunting season. It was a strange combo to anyone from anywhere else. But in Widow's Bay, it worked. Though it wasn't exactly a model that other struggling independent book-stores could emulate.

"Let me send some Cold Comfort home with you," Tatum said.

"Do I want to know?"

"It's miraculous. No one has time to be sick these days, and it works in what? Twelve hours?" Fawn added.

"Yep. I sent some to your Aunt last week for the sniffles she had," Tatum said to me.

"Great."

"Don't worry I'm learning to temper my special brews, so they don't upset the balance of the universe."

"They totally could," Fawn said.

"Let's get moving, I have a conference call with Brule on the Yule Days thing. You know he can only do business at night. That's annoying by the way, but what are you going to do?" Candy said, and everyone let it go. Nocturnal business meetings were ordinary now. We were getting used to the new normal in Widow's Bay.

"We need to be in a good circle." We all sat in the chairs and watched as tiny bubbles simmered in the cauldron.

"So what? We just start?" I was the least experienced witch of the bunch.

"Temperature has to be right," Georgie said and looked to Tatum.

"Ten seconds," Tatum said, and we watched as the steam escaped the brew and the pace of the bubbles quickened. I watched Pauline stare at the cauldron and realized she was providing the intensity for the task that we needed.

Tatum nodded toward Georgianne. It was go time.

"Fawn, add the item." Fawn leaned over to Candy and looked intently at Candy's perfectly coiffed blonde bob. Fawn gently pulled a single hair free and then yanked.

"Ow!"

"Sorry, normally we need animal or herb or whatever, but for this one, since it's mischief against you, we needed a part of you. I thought hair would be better than blood or nails. You just got the gel manicure."

"Thanks." Candy put a hand up and smoothed the hair mussed by Fawn's plucking.

Fawn looked to Tatum and Tatum held up a hand to halt her for a second. We waited for the go ahead. Tatum put her hand down, and Fawn carefully leaned over the cauldron. The glow of the flame below it illuminated Fawn's pretty skin and dark hair in a way that made me envious of her gene pool. She really did look like a queen. Brule had saved the witches of the tribes that lived here before even him, indigenous people, Fawn's people. The timeline to all of it was murky and ancient, and incomprehensible.

"Okay, we all need to hold hands. Marzie, you go when Tatum says."

I swallowed hard. I was crossing a line here now. I'd done things, I had powers. I'd made things happen. I knew that. But before, it was emotion and impulse. I'd summoned help when I thought I was going to die. I'd shoved Kayleigh with my rage. There wasn't premeditation to any of it. There wasn't planning or intent. There was danger, and instinct, and emotion, and it had worked every time.

But this time, I was deliberately making magic. Could I? Would this really work?

Georgie had instructed me that this spell needed to reveal mischief or harmful intent. And it would only work if the harm was coming from other magic. If people were just talking smack, well, that was life, and we may not see a thing.

Part of me wanted the spell to fail. I was walking across the last threshold of normal. And part of me wanted it to succeed. I wanted to learn what I could do. I wanted to use my power to help my friend, to help the town, and even to help Brule like he believed I could. I wanted to believe that this vision of me, this version of me, this self-assured wielder of magical forces, was true.

The simmer in the cauldron graduated to a full boil. And there was something else. There were little flickers of light, sparks I guess, floating up in the steam that rose from the liquid. The rest of the Frog Toe ignored us, going about their business as if another spell was at work on them. Or maybe they all knew not to interfere with whatever was coming through we six around the cauldron.

Tatum nodded to me. I took a breath and swallowed.

A NASTY WORD
> That rumor's feed.
> A mean intent
> Turning straight to bent.
> One who is pure in deed and action
> Withstands attacks from an evil faction.
> Show us now, whose words do her harm.
> Reveal the face and the twisted charm!

MY VOICE WAS LOW, powerful, and different to my own ears. The words left my mouth like they had a form of their own. They hung over the cauldron and slid into the heated liquid just as Candy's hair had entered the pot.

We watched as steam rose and swirled. It held us all in rapt attention.

Something was happening. Something more than me reciting a poem. The six of us continued to hold hands. The vapor began to collect. It seemed to organize itself, soft edges turned harder, more defined. The air was thick with the smell of wood burning. The little sparks that rose glittered and danced.

"Oh, oh my," Pauline said, and I began to see what she did. The steam transformed into an image.

I saw a man taking money. Bills were being pressed into his hands. It was like we were watching an image projected on water or clouds. The man was handsome, dark, he wore clothes that did not look like they belonged in Widow's Bay, or even in this decade.

The image rotated. We saw clearly who was giving the dark man the bills.

It was Ridge Schutte.

"I knew it," Candy hissed under her breath.

"Shh," Georgianne said. We watched a second more, trying to decipher exactly what was happening. But the slightest wind from Candy's breath shifted the steam over the cauldron. The image dissipated.

The tight bond of magic that held us together loosened its grip. But we remained in our places. We sat, silent, as though we were unable to move after watching the end of an epic movie. The credits were rolling, but we were still in our seats. Finally, Pauline spoke.

"I said it all along, Ridge Schutte is evil, but I thought he was normal evil, I didn't think he had any magic," Pauline said as we tried to process what we had seen.

"He doesn't, but that man he paid does," I said. I didn't know how I knew it, but I did.

"Yep, so that's your answer Candy. That snake Ridge, who just can't stand all the magical tourism you're bringing in, is contract hiring spells against you," Georgie said, interpreting what we'd just witnessed. I could argue that we didn't really know that's what we saw. That we were all novices in casting a spell this way much less deciding what the images really meant. Except I had the exact same impression of what we'd just seen.

"Is that spell he paid that guy for a rumor spell? We can do a rumor spell?" Candy asked.

"Yes. I think it is. That's what we saw. I mean if I can brew a stout that helps someone win at Keno, there must be a way to conjure something to feed the rumor mill that you're buying foreign cars," Tatum said.

"Well let's fight back! Can we do a counterspell, start rumors about him?" Pauline proposed an obvious solution.

I had no idea if that was possible. Though I had no confidence that today's spell would work, and it apparently had.

"You cannot." It was a voice outside our circle. But it was familiar. We all turned to see a formidable little woman whose last statement was not a question but a firm command.

"Aunt Dorothy!"

"That's one of your cardinal rules ladies. We don't use spells to hurt others or the town. Especially pompous fools like Ridge Schutte, it's the fastest way to turn into bitter, evil, old Lottie Bradbury. And there's a price to pay for summoning ill will to deal with non-magical types," Dorothy said as she stepped into our circle.

"So how the heck am I going to win this election?" Candy said to the universe, more than to any of us present.

"The old-fashioned way, kissing babies, and making sure we get those Union endorsements." Aunt Dorothy injected a dose of practicality into our magical night. Aunt Dorothy and practicality, now that was magic.

CHAPTER 10

I wanted to see the paint in the morning light, that was what you were supposed to do. I'd seen it on HGTV.

The dining room was situated in the front of the house, off the foyer. I had agreed to give it over to Agnes and Bubba once it was done. In exchange, Agnes was going to let me fix it up. Agnes was not, however, going to let me fix it up without her design consultation. And by consultation, I meant precise control over all decorating decisions.

I'd gotten up early and was studying the paint samples. They all looked sort of right? And sort of wrong.

"You've managed to bring home, literally, fifty shades of gray. If ever there was a cry for help that is it."

Agnes sauntered in and joined me in staring at the paint samples.

"Very funny." That I spoke to Agnes out loud and she talked to me in my head was something I now accepted as normal. Whether anyone who saw this interaction thought I was nuts didn't concern me. In Widow's Bay talking out loud to your cat was so low on the wackadoo scale it barely moved the needle.

"That one's too green, this row is nearly white, that one is too blue.

Pick the classic silver gray and tell your hound to be very careful with the white trim."

"His name is Grady, and you promised to stay out of the way today and let him work."

"I've decided to spend the day in the library. Bubba has been instructed to growl at any other canines who enter."

That was fine. They'd be out of the way and my hound, uh, Grady, could do the dining room work he needed. I looked at the classic silver-gray paint Agnes had just selected.

"Damn, she's right." It was the best one, no question.

I was feeling accomplished. The paint had been selected. I'd also negotiated a neutral zone for my pets, so Grady could work without incursions or feline protests.

I was about to head out to get to work when a commotion erupted in my driveway.

Two men, almost as big as Grady, were hollering at each other and pushing each other chest to chest. It had been several days since a fight had broken out in Widow's Bay, so I supposed we were overdue. I just didn't expect this one to happen at my house.

It was early in the day, in my quiet neighborhood, and they were working up to a shouting match. I saw curtains flutter in a window across the street.

If I didn't get this one simmered down fast, I'd likely be begging Loof not to charge me with disturbing the peace.

The two men were now full on shouting.

As I got closer, I could see, that while they were men, they were young.

"I am sick of your driving. You start and stop and start and it makes me want to hurl," said one of the hotheads. He was a big boy, over six foot, but wiry. He had a scruffy brown beard but was still young looking, I pegged him in his early twenties.

"Did you ever think the beer you had last night made you want to hurl?" The other one was a little smaller, lighter. He had sandy blonde hair. He may be smaller, but not by much, and he was holding his ground.

"You're not here to tell me what to do, little brother!" The one with the beard fired back. Confirmation of what I'd suspected. The fight looked like a brother fight. I'd seen my share of those. Sometimes with brothers you just let them go at it. It usually tired everyone out with no significant harm done. But these two could both do some damage to each other and anyone who happened to wander into the melee. The verbal battle was about to turn physical, so I quickened my step.

"Hey. Hey." I put the hardest edge I could to my voice. Then I stepped in between the two. They could both squish me like a bug, but I was going to bluff. I expected them to be shocked that a little old lady would order them around. Hopefully shocked enough to cool down and take it somewhere else.

"Who the hell are you?" the bigger one said.

"Excuse me? I'm going to do you both a favor. This is a nice and quiet neighborhood, and I'm pretty sure most of my neighbors are about to call the cops if you don't put an end to your slap fest."

"It's none of anyone's business," said the beardless one. The temperature between the two hadn't cooled even a degree since I'd interrupted. But I didn't summon help. This was familiar territory, two near men, fighting over something stupid. This I could deal with.

"Really? You're in my driveway so I'd say it's my business."

I keep my voice low and calm. I was never one to yell at my boys in public. It always makes the yeller look insane when it's out of context. I tried the same on these two. I pretended that I was in complete control. Though at this point they could have both picked me up and drop kicked me. But as I suspected, they were stunned into silence by my audacious assertion of authority.

That's when I knew from experience to push my advantage. I

squared my shoulders and put a palm on the chest of the younger one. He was worked up for sure. His heart practically jumped out of his t-shirt, and his skin was almost hot to the touch. It nearly threw me off the reason I was standing in between the two. With a hand on the young, beardless one, I swiveled my head to the older one.

"You appear to be older. Show a good example of how to behave on a job site." I was freestyling. I had deduced this was Grady's crew. The bigger one looked enough like Grady to make me wonder if he had a dozen sons or what?

My motherly boss voice worked. "Yes, ma'am. We apologize. We forgot ourselves."

Both men stepped back and actually started to bow a little to me. That's right.

That's when Grady arrived on the scene. I hadn't even heard his truck pull up.

"Braden! Finn! What's going on?"

"We got into it because he doesn't listen," Finn, the older bearded one, said.

"He can't stop giving orders, and he drives for sh--," Braden, the clean-shaven younger one, fired back but

Grady walked up and grabbed the bigger of the two, Finn, by the ear, before he could finish.

"Ow. Uh yes. We're sorry."

I nodded and accepted the apology.

For a change, Grady seemed to be stunned by me instead of vice versa.

"Go get the supplies I just bought. Put down a tarp, so you don't track your dirt into the nice lady's house." The sweet demeanor I'd seen with little Crad was replaced by a much gruffer one with these two. The man-children hung their heads and headed for Grady's truck.

"I didn't see the entire event but what I did see is rather dangerous, stepping in between two young men about to rip each other's heads off. I estimate you to be about 115 pounds." Grady flattered me and also seemed genuinely worried.

"I'm used to handling unruly beasts remember? And yes I'm exactly 115 pounds." Which was true in maybe 1990 and twenty pounds ago.

"Let me apologize for them as well. I'm ashamed of them."

"I think they're good boys, maybe just spirited?"

"Yes, spirited."

"They're clearly related to you. How?"

"In my pack, my brother's kids. My problem now." The resemblance was now explained.

"Why is that?" There was a dark shadow over Grady's face. I had maybe stepped into a territory that was too personal.

"He died right before the gate was opened. Hunted."

"Oh."

"Yeah, he was the alpha, I am now, which means a lot of work to do with them to show them how to act. You seemed to handle it well though, a regular den mother."

"Ha, I was an actual den mother at one point."

"I can't promise it won't happen again, but they're good with floor stripping, refinishing, and edging."

"What's a little brotherly brawl if they're good contractors?"

"Apprentice contractors. We're working on it. Best get them into the logging business, into the woods, and out of the nice neighborhoods of Widow's Bay before they get arrested."

"Probably a good idea. Agnes has selected the paint color by the way. It's on the fridge. Do you need me to pick it up?"

"No, we'll get the paint going and then the floor. It will be done before you're home from work if I can keep them from killing each other."

"Well, if they do, try to make sure they do it on that tarp." I laughed.

"See, you're a good den mother, you appreciate that a certain amount of wrestling and bloodshed comes with the territory. I wonder if you could help me with… uh, no, too much."

"What?"

"Uh, Crad, school, we're having an issue with the teacher. I have no idea how to deal with that."

"Teacher's meeting for a rowdy little boy?" I had been at my share of those too.

"Sorry, Crad's mom usually handled the finer points." I wanted to help him. I also wondered what had happened to Crad's mother. But it wasn't a conversation to have on the way to work or in passing.

"My advice? Tell the teacher to keep your boy busy, errands, jobs, projects, the more, the better. It will keep him out of trouble. Plus, I met Craddock, he wants to help. Tell the teacher that about him."

"Thanks."

"Yep, have a good day. Help yourself to the coffee in the pot."

I know Grady was watching me as I walked to my Jeep. I felt it. There was something so alluring about a man trying to be a good Dad. I shook it off. While Brule was all intense connection and reminding me that I was intertwined with some historical destiny in Widow's Bay, Grady was fun. Though Grady's brood was a lot furrier than I supposed my two actual sons were, navigating testosterone, even part-canine, was in my wheelhouse. And a heck of a lot less weighty then managing the history of vampires and witches. The monsters in my life were at both ends of the spectrum it seemed.

How I'd managed to go from divorced empty nester to considering supernatural options in dating, I'd never fully understand. I just hoped my house was in one piece and Agnes steered clear for the day.

My mission for today was Keith Foley.

The last time anyone had seen Earl he was having coffee with

Foley. By just about everyone's account, Earl was a recluse and coffee in town wasn't his normal routine.

I headed to Maggie's Diner in hopes of tracking him down. Apparently, he was a regular.

The smell of bacon, eggs, and perfection at Maggie's made my mouth water. Most mornings, I chugged my coffee and got to work. I'd spent my adult life trying not to eat. It was sad actually, now that I really thought about it. There was no reason to deprive myself to please a news consultant or for fear a camera would add ten pounds.

I walked up to the counter. The room was full. It looked like a healthy mix of tourists and regulars

"Hi, I'm looking for Keith Foley. I was told he's a regular," I said to the waitress.

"Yep, Keith's right there, regular booth." I followed her eyes, and there he was. He wore khakis and white button-down shirt. His coat was wadded up on the booth next to him. He was deeply engrossed in something on his phone.

"Thanks."

I plastered a smile on my face and approached.

"Hi, Keith Foley? I'm Marzie Nowak, from Your U.P News, wondered if I could share a booth with you for a second?" Keith smiled back and then looked around. If I were going to characterize the look I'd say it was nervous. It was a common response to being approached by a reporter, no matter what the reason.

"Uh, sure. I recommend the omelet!"

"Thanks."

"I enjoyed your story on Samhain Slopes." Keith Foley was soft in the middle and at the chin. He was clean-shaven and didn't have much hair. But the hair he did have was artfully arranged on top. I ventured the hair design fooled no one.

"Exclusives with Stephen Brule are hard to come by, I appreciate that."

"You're from here right?"

"Yes, back after a long stint in Detroit."

"Sure, sure, lived in Mount Pleasant for a while but fell in love with a local so here we are."

"Ha, that will do it."

"Yeah, wife, two kids, nice house in the Green Hills neighborhood, got it right before the housing collapse."

"Wow cool, so that logo there, isn't that PureLiquid?" I recognized the brand, it was a big company.

"Yes. Bingo."

"I didn't know they were here in Michigan. Don't they sell that Clear Fuel Hydration drink all the athletes chug?"

"Yes, that's our big seller, but we're expanding all over."

"So, Michigan?"

"Yes, they approached me to help out. Since I'm a native."

"Got it. I don't want to intrude on your day, but I'm doing a follow-up story on the death of Earl McGowan."

"Oh, so sad, I heard about that. He was getting pretty frail." Keith Foley shook his head, and the corners of his mouth turned down in what I guessed was sadness.

"I heard you were one of the last ones to see him."

"Really? I didn't know that."

"Yeah, here, in fact."

Keith widened his eyes in surprise, then he bit his lower lip, narrowed his eyes, and then nodded as he recalled the event I mentioned.

"Yes, that's right, we had lunch."

"So, you were friends?"

"No, business associates."

"What type of business?"

"He's got a great natural spring on the Northeast section of his property. That's what we were working on."

"What do you mean?"

"We worked about a deal to get the rights to a really delicious and pure natural spring for the next generation of water."

"You're going to be selling water from here through PureLiquid?"

"Bottled straight from Pure Michigan to PureLiquid, Earl loved that phrase when I ran it by him."

"I thought you had to get approval from, well, somewhere, to do something like that?"

Keith squirmed a little and fiddled with his cellphone. It seemed awkward in his hands but at the same time a part of them. The phone beeped and his thumbs went flying.

I was clearly not in his focus when his cell phone beckoned, I bet the wife loved that.

"Shoot. Ugh. Oh sorry, just lost that one."

"You're playing a game?"

"Yeah totally addicted to this thing," he waved his phone. Now that the game was over he re-engaged in our conversation.

"Yeah, well, I don't handle government approvals, I was just there to show Earl what a great opportunity he had on his land."

"Had you seen Earl, out at his farm, after that breakfast you had here?"

"Ah, no, just here two weeks ago. He signed off on us doing the testing, which went great and things are full speed ahead. It's an exciting partnership."

"Between you and the dead farmer?"

"Oh, well, that's unfortunate that he won't see the water bottled. Samples are ready to be sent! Wow, that is sort of sad." Keith Foley broke eye contact and looked down at his phone again. He did not look sad. He looked distracted.

"I still keep thinking you'd need approval from, well, some government body, not just Earl to do that kind of deal?"

"Oh, no, only from Earl, God rest his soul."

"God rest his soul, and you saw him what day?"

"That would have been, here, like I said, two weeks ago. I was out to the farm, gosh, in the summer, but that was it." Keith Foley's phone beeped again. I leaned over and saw that he had some phone game going again. It was rude considering I was trying to have a conversation with him. Though I had interrupted his breakfast. Something about the entire thing was just weird.

"Well then thanks, I appreciate your help."

"Sure. Nice to meet you." He smiled at me, and I nodded.

"Quick question how much did PureLiquid pay Earl for those water rights?"

"Oh, gosh, that's not, uh, well, maybe you need to check in with corporate on that. Above my pay grade."

"But wouldn't you have to have a ballpark, to do the negotiating?"

"Gosh, I'd love to talk more, but I've got to hop on a conference call." Translation, Keith Foley was done talking to me.

"Sure, thanks for the chat."

The encounter was interesting, enlightening, and made me wonder if there was more to Earl McGowan's failing farm then met the eye.

And it also made me wonder how a damn cell phone game could completely obsess an adult male. Or, like many adult males, Keith was using the game to get out of adulting as the kids call it.

I slid out of the booth and left the odd salesman to his cell phone game.

It was time to head out to Earl's farm again.

CHAPTER 11

"What are you thinking for today," Justin asked as I touched base with him on my way back out to the McGowan farm.

"Checking out the McGowan Farm, then I'm not sure."

"Something new out there?"

"No, not really. Just some follow up. Also, the water level out there's low. I think I might know why or have a hunch. Could be an entirely new story. Do you know anything about PureLiquid trying to bottle water from the U.P.?"

"Yeah, a little, they were shooed out of Traverse City."

"Interesting. This is probably not a today story, I'd need to do some research."

"Okay, let me know what you do today by one or so."

"Yep."

It had snowed overnight. The Jeep tires crunched the fresh coat underneath the treads. The snow felt dry, which I'm sure is an oxymoron, dry snow. But it was and when it came to snow consistency dry snow was easier to drive on than wet snow or ice. It truly was like powder.

I looked toward Samhain Slopes. The weather had cooperated

with the launch of the new resort. Tourists were discovering the winter wonderland that encased our peninsula three seasons of the year. If you could handle the cold, you could spend your life on the slopes. Which for skiers, was paradise. Unlike the Rockies or European Alps, the sun didn't warm a skier on the slopes here. And cloud cover hovered over the mountain on most days.

I drove out to the country, past the small neighborhoods that hovered near Main Street, past the high school, and as far out as you could get in Widow's Bay.

Earl's driveway was long. Seewhy pond sat at the front of the property. Earl's land was partially obscured by a tree line at the road. I didn't see any evidence of the police emergency vehicles that had been there, the snow had covered the tracks and the mess they'd made.

I wondered if Tatum would eventually have to deal with Earl's estate. As of yet, no one had found a will.

I parked my Jeep, wound my new scarf around my neck, and walked up to the porch. The house was buttoned up tight. I peeked into a window, it was dark inside.

"What happened to you, Earl? Did you have a heart attack or a stroke?"

The wind howled around the porch, and I swore I heard the word, "No!" It startled me.

There was a desolate feel out here. The distance between homes, the wind, the fact that nature was untamed made you feel like you could be standing on the porch now or standing on the porch in a century gone by. All of Widow's Bay had that feeling now and again, come to think of it.

Had the ghost of Earl McGowan yelled no? I wondered. I had seen quite a few visions lately, could I be hearing them now too?

I looked around.

I decided to walk to the back of Earl McGowan's property. He had a lot of it, and according to Keith Foley, they were already working out here, to pump the water and bottle it to sell. It still seemed odd to me that a company could just take water from one place and sell it without a public outcry or at least a vote.

I pulled up the hood of my knee-length parka. I would get used to the cold, I knew that, over time. Like a sailor had sea legs, I'd find my cold legs, but I hadn't yet.

I opened the GPS app on my phone and pulled up the McGowan farm. I angled myself Northeast. Keith said the spring was located there and that was also where Lake Superior bordered Earl's farm. The lake helped stir up the wind. Great.

I walked less than five minutes when it was clear that the voice I'd heard shouting no probably wasn't old Earl from the great beyond.

Four commercial trucks were parked on the land, and men were standing around them. The trucks looked like they could dig and maybe pump stuff? There were giant hoses and a tank on two of them. And sure enough, there was that PureLiquid Logo again.

A man in a tan Carhartt style work jumpsuit and a safety orange ski hat stood toe to toe with another man.

The second man looked less equipped for the weather conditions. His coat was long, burgundy, and was embroidered with a tapestry pattern. It had a white fur collar. His ink black, shoulder length hair waved in the wind. There were people, similarly dressed, maybe a dozen, hovering around the edge of the scene.

I quickened my pace. I was focused on the standoff in front of me, but as I got closer, I saw that people were lying in front of the wheels of the commercial vehicles.

I'd stumbled into a protest.

I clicked from my GPS app to the video camera and hit record. If anything looked like an exclusive story, this did.

"You will not be drilling on this land." The dark-haired man looked like he'd wandered away from an anti-war protest in 1972 and straight into this scene. The wind blew his hair around his face and danced like tongues of dark flames.

"We have a permit. It's signed." The man in the work coat waved a piece of paper in front of him.

"We will not be moved."

I walked closer. There had to be a half-a-dozen people lying in front of the vehicles. The rest were standing firm in solidarity behind the dark-haired leader of this protest.

"This water is sacred and not yours."

"This water is the property of PureLiquid, and unless you want their corporate attorneys up your hippie butt, you'll move."

"This is what is known. We will not move. You may crush us with your steel wheels. The souls of my people will haunt you and your issue to the end of days!"

Well, yikes.

The man with the paperwork didn't have a similar eternal curse to hurl in response.

"Fine, tomorrow we'll be out here with the cops. Scotty, pack it up."

"Bring all your legions! We will be victorious!"

"Whatever you're smoking you need to dial it back a little," said the foreman in the Carhartt, apparently more annoyed than afraid of the curses and theatrics.

Now was my opportunity to get some actual interviews, before they drove off.

"Sir, I'm Marzie Nowak, Your U.P. News, what's PureLiquid trying to do out here?"

"Call corporate's Media Relations department. I'm not allowed to talk to reporters."

"I just need you to tell me what you're doing out here."

"Nothing today lady. As you can see the roadshow for Hair has decided to perform for us."

The crew all got in their trucks, and the dark-haired man made a motion with his hands. The people lying in protest got up and joined the larger group standing in defiance against PureLiquid.

The foreman offered a middle finger salute to the roadshow of Hair, as he'd dubbed the collection of protestors. The protestors responded in kind. Lovely all around.

It wasn't until the trucks were in motion that the leader and chief curse hurler looked in my direction.

"You, you're with the news?"

"I am."

"Did you get all that with your iPhone?"

It was weird that a man who'd just invoked an eternal haunting knew I had a smartphone.

"Yep."

"Great. That will help. You better make sure that thing goes viral."

"I need to ask you a few questions. For the story."

"Sure, walk with us. It's frigging cold out here sister."

The man waved me forward. His followers, or whatever they were, turned and led the way.

"I'm Marzie Nowak. Your U.P. News."

"Yeah, I heard. So, here's the story."

I interrupted, I had no idea who this man was.

"Your name? Can I get your name? And I'm recording okay?"

"Sure, yeah, I'm Giles Johnne Blyth Faa."

"Um, a lot of names there."

"Johnne has two n's and an e. And Faa has two a's. Call me Giles."

"Okay, and you're with an environmental group or something?"

"No, I'm the Gypsy King, but don't print that. Tell them that Boswell over there is the king."

"King? Which one's Boswell."

"The one who was laying under the tanker wheels. It's best for the organization if the police try to arrest Boswell, not me."

"Oh, sure, of course." I had run into shifters, trolls, vampires, why not travelers?

"We're back, and this land isn't for sale to the corporations. You know?"

"Well, technically it might be. The farmer Earl McGowan? He may have signed over the water rights."

"That's not his to do."

"Uh, well, yes, it is."

"Land can't be owned, when will you see that?"

"Uh, okay, so why don't you want the drilling?"

"For the purpose of your news story let me say this. This water is the birthright of the land we stand on. This water is ours who live on this land. This water is how all of us live and thrive here. It isn't a commodity that one cold corporation can commercialize and profit from. It's a natural resource provided by Mother Earth to nurture the creatures here, not hydrate the idiots who live in deserts."

"Okay. Got it."

"Official interview over." Giles, the self-proclaimed under cover Gypsy King, stopped walking. I followed the direction of his eyes. There were RVs, pup tents, and bonfires going in the distance. They'd erected a small community here on the edge of Earl McGowan's land.

"So, I'm going to write the protest story, you're doing this for everyone who lives here?" I asked.

"The Upper Peninsula has a wealth of natural riches. But it is a rugged place. Remote. Our reward for the hardship is clean water. It's not for sale."

"Okay, got it, on the record, right."

"Yes."

"Off the record, that curse?"

"Oh, yeah? You heard that?"

"Yes."

"Put it in the story if you want but it will make us look crazy, and our cause isn't crazy."

"Okay." I struggled with exactly what to make of this Gypsy

King and his mission.

"Know this, my people need this water, it is tied to our life in a way no other water is. We'll do everything we must to preserve access to it. It will not be drained for thirty pieces of silver."

Giles looked into my eyes. His were smoldering, intense, and a little wild. And there was something familiar. I'd seen him somewhere. I knew I had.

I searched my memory while I felt him searching my face. I felt we were both trying to decide what to make of the other. As a reporter, I tried to stay neutral. It wasn't a reporter's job to take sides. As a person, the magnetism of this man was off the chart. It had to be if he could incite people to lie down under the wheels of the massive equipment.

"The story will be online later today." That was all I could think of to say.

"Cool. I'll share it on our Facebook page." Of course, the travelers had a Facebook page.

Then it struck me where I'd seen his face. Where I had just seen this exact face!

He was the one we'd seen in the smoke during our spell. He was the one making a deal with Ridge Schutte.

The man who was trying to derail Candy's campaign with rumor and innuendo was standing in front of me.

And I had no idea what to do next.

Self-preservation took over. I was surrounded by a group of people who I didn't know. Who may or may not be able to curse my progeny for the rest of time.

Confronting him now, over magic I didn't understand, seemed ill-advised.

I decided to make my goodbye.

I was writing the story about the protest in my head as I made my way back to the Jeep. I also had calls to make to flesh out the details of what had happened out here, but my mind was racing.

Something more than a suspicious death investigation was unfolding on McGowan's land.

I filed away the revelation that the Gypsy King of Widow's Bay was politicking with Ridge Schutte. I'd need to share that revelation with the coven.

A dead body, corporate intrigue, a fight over natural resources, a protest, and a Gypsy curse. This was all before lunch.

CHAPTER 12

*P*rotestors bar workers from tapping spring at McGowan's Farm

Widow's Bay, MI

Over a dozen protestors put their bodies in front of four commercial vehicles on a farm in the northeast section of rural Widow's Bay.

The property, owned by the late Earl McGowan, was the scene of a showdown between contractors and a group led by Giles Johnne Blyth Faa.

"This company thinks they can transport 200 gallons of water a minute out of a well on private property. It is a raping of the land, and we're here to stop it."

Workers on the scene did not comment on the situation but directed inquiries to PureLiquid, Inc.

Daphne Duckense, spokesperson for All Continental Unlimited, parent company of PureLiquid, issued this statement to Your U.P. News.

"PureLiquid has obtained legal approval from the Chippewa County Branch of the Michigan Department of Environmental Quality to legally proceed with extracting water from the McGowan spring. The company went through all the official legal and proper channels and has received permitting to do so. PureLiquid is and will continue to be

committed to being a shining example of a good corporate citizen. Pure-Liquid Beverages is a trusted brand and thanks to the beautiful sparkling water at the McGowan spring families throughout the country will enjoy the pure, clean taste originating in Northern Michigan. The company seeks to continue to keep an open dialogue with residents, customers, and all stake holders."

Faa countered, "Corporations do not own that water, it is as absurd as claiming to own the sky."

Local officials were surprised to learn PureLiquid had secured approval from the landowner and the Michigan DEQ.

"It is my understanding that public comment is required for such an action," said Council Woman Candy Hitchcock.

In a rare instance of agreement between political rivals, Hitchcock's opponent in the upcoming mayoral race, Councilman Ridge Schutte, concurred that the public should weigh in on the matter.

"Something is off on this," said Schutte.

Work was halted and the protestors, now apparently camping on a portion of the farmland, say they will return if the work resumes.

The spokesperson for PureLiquid said the company was not pressing charges over the incident but would do so if any further obstruction occurred.

"Nice. How the heck does a major corporation get government approval to suck the water out without anyone knowing a thing about it?" Justin had called after I filed my story.

"I don't know. Worth a few questions I think. Earl McGowan may not have been able to grow any decent crops out on that farm, but it turns out it's fertile ground for news."

"Good one, yeah, keep at it. Great work -- love this exclusive." Justin and I hung up.

I thought again about Giles Johnne Blyth Faa, the Gypsy King. What business did he have with Ridge Schutte?

And if travelers were Yooper Naturals, what were their powers?

Every question led to a dozen more.

Questions were my business, and I had a bumper crop right now.

I noticed my gas was low after filing my story so a stop over to Holiday Gas was in order. It was further out of town than the gas station on Main, but I liked Seyed better than Gail Keener, owner of the BP on main. He had better gossip and had better coffee.

I filled the tank, and then headed in to grab my coffee and maybe whatever tidbits I could.

"Good afternoon Marzie!" Seyed was always stocking, cleaning, or chatting. I had never seen him stand still for more than a second. I'd caught him filling the coffee maker.

"You'll have the first cup from this fresh brew."

"Sounds like perfect timing. How are you?"

"Well, doing well, thank you. What do you hear about the Earl McGowan situation. Suspicious eh? How do they figure that? Stabbed before the car went into the pond? Shot?" I paid for my news tips from Seyed with information he could share with his customers. It was a good arrangement.

"No, he didn't have water in his lungs. When you drown, that's what happens, you suck in water instead of air." Seyed nodded in understanding and then went about filling the cup holder next to the coffee pot.

"Stroke? Heart attack?"

"They're looking for that now." Then it dawned on me, Seyed was in a position to observe a lot of people's driving habits.

"Seyed, you see every kind of driver here."

"Yes, some who shouldn't be drivers at all if I had anything to say about it."

"People mostly wear their seatbelts?"

"I'd say yes, that beeping noise is like a nagging crone, no offense."

Apparently, my reputation as a witch was now making the rounds.

"None taken."

"What kind of people don't wear seatbelts?"

"The very old, the very young, and the very stubborn. Which is usually the old and the young."

"Earl was wearing his when his car went in the pond, but I heard he was firmly in that not going to wear a seatbelt camp."

"Is that a clue?"

"Not sure, just a running it by you."

"Hmm, people are either one or the other, like smokers, that I do know."

"That's what I think too."

"Large?" Seyed asked as he grabbed a to go cup. I probably shouldn't have an afternoon cuppa joe, but an afternoon pick-me-up might help me think clearly about how the day had gone.

"Please."

"So, did you talk to your friend Fawn yet today?"

"No, saw her last night." Sayed clearly had information to share.

This made me immediately nervous. When you do news in Detroit you rarely did a story that involved friends or family since it was a big city. In Widow's Bay every story seemed to lead to friends of family or naked bear shifters or Sasquatch research.

"I guess there was a little issue out at her vet clinic last night after she'd left for the night. Maybe worth calling her."

"But everyone's okay?"

"Oh, I just heard there was a break in. The kid who works there stopped in to fill up their van right before you stopped in. He got a call to get over there fast and I just happened to hear."

"Thanks, Seyed. I'll check it out." I paid for my coffee and hustled out to the Jeep.

I dialed Fawn's cell.

"What happened? Are you okay?"

"I'm okay. But I think you need to see for yourself. We may need that Liaison thingy you do."

"On the way."

I drove to Fawn's clinic as fast as possible without hitting vacationing pedestrians. It really was strange to have to even worry about traffic here.

I pulled into the vet clinic. The front window was gone and had been replaced with particle board. I raced inside.

Tyler, one of Fawn's vet tech assistants, was at the front desk. Normally it was Savanah, Fawn's young, sweet, and adorable receptionist, who greeted visitors.

"Exam Four, Dr. Campana said to send you right back."

"Thanks."

I broke into a sprint. Something felt incredibly wrong. I got to exam room four and lightly knocked.

"Come in."

I pushed open the door and found Fawn sitting next to a cot. Savanah, the sweet young receptionist, was laying on said cot.

"Oh my goodness, what happened?" I walked to the bed and stood next to Fawn. Worry wrinkled her brow.

"Savanah locked up last night, after I'd gone. This morning I came in and the window was smashed. Savanah's roommate called in and said Savanah was going to be late, she was under the weather.

"I called Loof, told him nothing was taken, and it wasn't an emergency. But then she comes in, about an hour ago. She says she was here when the window broke and there was a man. But that's as far as her story goes. She can't remember anything else. She got weirder and weirder and I made her lay down here."

"I'm fine. I just need to rest a little." Savanah said and offered a weak smile to us. She closed her eyes and drifted off less than a second later.

Fawn whispered to me.

"Look." Fawn brushed a lock of Savanah's blonde hair away from her neck. A gasp escaped my lips. There on Savanah's pale neck were two circular puncture marks.

"Are those what I think they are?"

"I think so."

"Okay, so yes on the Liaison thing."

It was almost 5 p.m. In the U.P. in December the sunsets happened before 5 p.m. It was 4:59. I hoped that meant Brule would hear me and could come, fast.

I put a gentle hand on Savanah's neck, where the skin had been pierced, I put my other hand in Fawn's.

"It can't hurt if we both call him. Think the words, come here, we need you." I instructed Fawn. I was surer of this power than the spell casting. I'd done it, it had worked.

I fixed Savanah's face firmly in my mind, then I thought of Brule and pushed out the message, "come here, we need you." I did it again.

Though sun had set it was not yet dark. I wondered if it was too soon, too early in the day. Fawn and I continued to hold hands. Savanah seemed to be struggling to stay awake.

I felt a shift in the air. I heard his voice behind me.

"Marzenna, are you safe?"

"I am."

I turned, and there he was in the doorway to the exam room, Etienne Brule.

Fawn and I stepped aside, and he entered; he had to duck a bit to clear the door. In a modern setting, in a small room, his broad shoulders filled the room. His size, whether he meant it or not, pushed us into the corners of the room.

"Who is this lamb?" He asked us.

"Fawn's receptionist. She said some man broke in last night, and well, look."

Brule kneeled at Savanah's side. He put a hand on her

forehead.

"She's cold, too cold," Brule said more to himself than to us.

"She was bitten right?" I said.

"Yes, and too much was taken."

"Like, is there a correct amount?" Fawn asked.

"There is a sip, a drink, and a draining and she iss dangerously past the drink stage."

"What does that mean? She's getting worse... do we need to call 911?" I asked.

"Medicine cannot help. She needs something else."

"What?" I knew the answer before he said it.

"She must drink from me."

"What will that do to her. Will it turn her?" Fawn asked with alarm in her voice.

"No, not if we only do this a single time. It will return her health, but--"

Brule stopped in mid-sentence.

"Yeah, go on." I was impatient, I was scared that Savanah may be suffering, and in danger.

"There is a consequence."

"What consequence?"

"If I do not give her my blood she will linger, half asleep, half-awake for the night, into the day, and then she either dies or lives. I cannot say which. But if it looks as if she will die at the end of that fight, it is too late to help."

"What?"

"I cannot reverse what has been done once the sun rises on day two."

"So, she could rally, overnight, or not, but you need to give her your blood by the second sunrise?"

"Yes. Or I can give her my blood now, restore her to health, but she will have a connection to me."

"Like what?

"She'll have to do my bidding, without fail. And she'll never be able to leave Widow's Bay. She won't be a vampire, but the price of the blood must be paid."

"Christ," I said out loud.

"She isn't in a position to decide. And she's getting weaker. Brule, you have to do this for her." Fawn was adamant. As Savanah lay there, it appeared she was getting paler, if that was possible. Fawn's instinct as a healer was in full flower, it didn't matter who or what was suffering. She wanted to fix it.

"She might get better. And what if she wants to leave?" I tried to run through the impact we were going to make on this woman's life. Forever.

"We can't gamble with her dying," Fawn said, and I didn't have a counter argument for that.

"Does she have a family we can call?"

"No," Fawn said. It was an awfully important decision we were being forced to make for Savanah, who now, was unconscious.

Fawn looked at me and in that moment, Savanah moaned. Her breath then became labored, every intake and exhale rattled with pain. This was new. It was the sign we needed. If we were betting on her getting better it would be a bad bet.

"Do it," Fawn said. Brule looked at us and nodded. His animal white teeth looked more pronounced than I'd ever noticed before.

He put his wrist to his mouth and slit it with his gleaming canine teeth. His eyes were locked on mine in that instant and I had the briefest flash of those same teeth, on my neck. Was it a memory from an ancestor or a premonition of what was to come? I didn't know.

The blood flowed from his wrist. He kneeled beside the cot and gently placed his wrist on Savanah's mouth. At first it appeared she was going to be smothered. I feared that we'd called a monster in to finish a monster's job. What had we done?

But then Savanah stirred, her hands locked onto Brule's

muscular forearm and she breathed in his blood like it was air. It lasted less than thirty seconds.

Brule extracted his arm gently and looked over to us. Fawn returned to Savanah's side. She smoothed the thick blonde hair away from Savanah's now-smooth brow.

"She will likely sleep until the next dawn. Bring her to me tomorrow at sunset. I will explain to her the new life she has." Brule instructed Fawn.

"I thought he was kind of cute. He had a North Face on." Savanah was mumbling to Fawn. Fawn nodded as though she was listening to delirium. But the North Face comment stopped me cold.

I looked at Brule. He ushered me into the hallway. My heart was now racing.

"That's the same one who attacked me. I thought you were going to talk to him."

"I have not been able to find him. Or his maker. But I will."

"Yeah, well you better make it fast. This jerk's on a feeding frenzy."

"Yes. And you were right to call me. You can see how important you are to me, to the town yes?"

I waved him off.

"It was obviously life or death." I had to remind myself about that. Maybe I'd have to remind myself about that for the rest of my life. Savanah would have a serious conversation with Brule, later, and I hoped she was okay. I hope she understood.

I put my hand on my eyebrows and rubbed them. I remembered the other questions floating around my brain and realized Brule might be able to help with at least with some of them.

"I have a question. What's the deal with travelers?"

"I advise not dealing with them if at all possible. They are skilled negotiators." As usual, Brule took my sentence a bit too literally.

"No, ugh, I mean what extra stuff can they do. Magic?"

"They have psychic abilities that they use for their own benefit, for money. It is distasteful."

"Well, isn't the resort, uh, well isn't profit the motive?"

"The resort is there to help give the entire town new prosperity. It provides stability. It is also important to have more population to..."

"Feed off of?" I glanced back at Savanah. I was angry to think that this new or ancient, depending on how you looked at it, population here in Widow's Bay had led to this innocent girl being attacked.

"No, but we need a diverse community to shelter all types of creatures." Brule looked at me.

"That sounds almost like a mission statement for a corporation."

"I do not understand."

"Forget it."

"I do not want to remind you about the oath your ancestors swore. The promise cannot be broken. Your people have made a pact, and in exchange, I will always do all I can to enrich this town. The resort is enriching. Your Candy understands. Profit is not my aim."

"Fine, fine," I said.

"But the travelers, that's different, profit is their aim."

"Well, Giles Faa, or whatever his name seemed to have a big family or community or whatever."

Brule made some sort of grunting sound in response. There were animosities, rivalries, and bad blood that stretched over hundreds of years. I was trying to get Brule to put it all in a nutshell. I wanted the bullet points about something that had unfolded before the country was even invented. Brule was not a bullet point kind of communicator.

"I will accompany you to your home. You should not be wandering around in town until I address this issue."

"Wandering? I have stuff to do. And you do need to address

the issue. If my deal is alerting you to trouble your deal needs to be keeping these blood suckers under control. Now go do that so I don't have to find this situation again." I was mad, madder than I'd been since I'd moved back home. It was frustrating to not understand things. It was infuriating to see a second attack from that same rogue vampire who Brule was supposedly handling.

Brule clenched his jaw. I turned and left the conversation. He wasn't the boss of me. No one was the boss of me.

I walked back to Fawn while Brule floated away or magically disappeared or turned into a bat or however he exited.

"How is she?"

"Her temperature is normal, she seems comfortable. I'm going to stay with her." Fawn said. She was a vet, that was true, but at heart she was a nurturer. I knew Savanah was in good hands.

"We did the right thing with Brule?" I asked Fawn and myself at the same time.

"We didn't have a choice, that I could see. It will be alright." Fawn said, and I nodded.

"I need to get home to Agnes and Bubba, and the werewolves who are redoing my dining room floor."

"That sentence represents real progress for you," Fawn said. She knew how much I had struggled accepting Yooper Naturals, and the whole kettle of fish we now swam in. I pulled her into a hug.

"I guess so, I mean the wolf in my dining room is pretty cute. Not a bad sight in the morning or after work."

"I thought you were more a vampire bride type?"

"Very funny. With the million stories I'm covering right now with Your U.P. News and Aunt Dorothy's antics my calendar is full. You need anything?"

"No, I'm fine. We'll be fine," Fawn said. Fawn was as competent a person as I'd ever met, as well as the most compassionate. She was honest, steadfast, generous, and she was my friend. I was so grateful for that fact.

I walked back to my Jeep. It was now fully dark in Widow's Bay.

Despite my bravado I did walk quickly to my car. I didn't want to attract anything that would be harmful to my neck. I didn't have time for it. And I didn't relish the idea of being at Brule's beck and call for all eternity. Though maybe I already was?

As I drove home I had the sense that a very familiar presence was following me. He watched from behind buildings, from above the trees. He was everywhere.

I knew Brule was hovering, I was sure I glimpsed a shock of white hair in my periphery, I had a distinct sense that he was nearby. It was a feeling I couldn't prove or describe if pressed.

He'd left me alone, as I'd asked. But he watched to be sure that I'd made it safely back home.

Men.

CHAPTER 13

I returned to a dining room that looked spectacular. Yay! Order and beauty at the end of a tumultuous day. From the paint to the refinished floor, it was stunning. There was a note from Grady stuck to my fridge.

"Onward to the kitchen, if you're brave enough. Let your feline empress know she can return to her realm in twenty-four hours when everything's dry. Grady."

Agnes padded in to find me reading the note.

"He's handsome. Has a nice butt. But honestly, go for the vampire. He's rich."

"I'm not dating Grady or Brule for that matter. Not that it's any of your business."

"Of course it's my business. And you need a blowout and touchup. Also, do you think your complexion is so glowing that you don't need a little blush? You're nearly as pale as that vampire without the gothic backstory."

Agnes padded away satisfied in the knowledge that she was correct about my relationships and my hair and makeup.

I looked at myself in the reflection of the microwave door. I was pale, and my gray streak was glowing. I had no idea when I'd have time to deal with that aspect of my life. Grooming. And I wasn't that worried about it. I knew Agnes wouldn't allow my standards to slip too far before she added her blistering advice.

My phone buzzed.

"Emergency meeting, after Zumba." It was the group text that Pauline had titled Coven Mitt. The Mitten was a nickname for Michigan, and she loved her little play on words.

"Yep, we all saw that traveler in your story," Georgie added to the thread.

"I'm researching fines and penalties for squatting." Candy was always at ready with a city ordinance for every occasion.

"Fill me in after your dance class, and eff that company trying to take our water," Tatum weighed in. She kept her muscle tone by lifting kegs. Morning Zumba wasn't ever going to be on her list of things to do.

"Fawn's going to miss too, she's got her hands full. I'll explain in the morning."

We all signed off. I crawled into my bed and closed my eyes. Gypsy Kings, water, and Earl McGowan battled in my brain with the sight of Brule saving Savanah.

I eventually fell asleep on my satin pillow case. But it was brief, light, and unsatisfying.

I showed up the next morning at Zumba with a half a belly full of caffeine but a full to the brim number of things to worry about.

"And shake your shoulders," Pauline said. We tried to comply with her dance instructions. She sported tennis shoes with light up soles. Pauline's enthusiasm powered a lot of us through class. As though her energy could get us through anything, even twerking. I, for the most part, was just trying not to die.

I had secured a space in the back of the class. I was bad at Zumba. Epically bad. But I wasn't alone. Georgie was also a Zumba idiot like me. We laughed our way through the class, sweated, and hoped Pauline wouldn't have the rest of the class turn around too much so the front would see what the back was doing. Or trying to do.

Candy, likely future mayor of Widow's Bay, could shake her hips, shoulders, and tailfeather in a way that made me wonder if she hadn't missed her calling as the next Shakira. I marveled at her Zumba prowess. It was no surprise that Pauline was good at this, but Candy?

Pauline's exercise class was always shifting. We'd finished four weeks of Spinning, and now we were in Zumba hell. I struggled to place my feet on the half beat and just hoped the next incarnation of this class would be something I could actually do. Though I'd heard Pauline talk about something called TRX and inwardly dreaded what that might entail.

The switch to Zumba had not deterred the new influx of male supernatural group fitness fans who now populated Widow's Bay. Bret, the bear shifter who loved fish tacos to a dangerous degree, was easily shimmying in the front of the class.

I believed that there is an unspoken foundational rule of the universe. If you're good at Zumba, you go in the front row. Even if you are a man/bear big enough to block the view of the instructor for the rest of the class. Good at Zumba, go in the front and leave the back row for the Zumba challenged so we could suffer in anonymity.

The good news about our friend Bret was it appeared that he had gotten his spontaneous shifting problem under control. The smell of fish tacos hadn't produced a traffic jam in several weeks. Good thing: if he got caught on camera again, he would throw the Bigfoot/Sasquatch society into a disarray from which they'd never recover. New koozies would need to be ordered, it would be a whole thing.

The class finished. The four members of the Coven Mitt group text adjourned to Pauline's real estate office conference room to discuss the recent developments.

We sucked down water and coffee as we hashed out the latest developments.

"That Giles Faa is trying to ruin my campaign!" Candy was livid, and though I didn't have a spare step in me after class, she was pacing around the conference room.

"The nerve!" Pauline agreed with Candy in all things.

"The question is why," said Georgie.

"The man's goal yesterday was to stop the water being removed. Does he think you're for the water sale or something?"

"Yeah, about that. Your article has ignited an uproar. There's universal outrage that a company could come in and take water from us to sell to the rest of the world."

"And how can they? How does PureLiquid have a state issued permit? Wouldn't there have to be public commentary?" I didn't know all laws of the county or the state but this one seemed obvious.

"I'm researching the rules, but I would say yes. I mean you can't paint a crosswalk without ten meetings that involve everyone who's ever lived in Widow's Bay," Candy said.

"Here's what we know," Georgie listed the issues. "The company seems to have a valid permit, wouldn't Earl have had to sign off? He was a real, uh, well he didn't seem like the kind of guy to make any deals or agree with anyone about anything."

"He signed off, I talked to a guy name Keith Foley. I guess he works for the water company, he got Earl to sign, told me so. Said it was official, and a done deal. Turns out he was one of the last people to actually see Earl. They had lunch." I shared the information I'd acquired in the course of my investigations for Your U.P. News.

"Our normal council meeting is tonight. I have to show that I'm against the water thing. It's a mess. It couldn't be worse timing, right in the final stages for planning Yule Days."

I knew what my story for the night would be at least. A town hall about selling Widow's Bay water to corporate outsiders was a news story, no question.

"And we also have a murder, maybe, of Earl McGowan," I added. This was still the top mystery in Widow's Bay right now in my book.

"Yeah, oh, and what are we all wearing for the Yule Ball thing," Pauline added to our list of questions. Outfits? She wanted to talk outfits.

Ugh.

We left our impromptu meeting with no clear idea of how to answer any of the questions we raised. Including the outfits.

It was still early when I got home to shower off the sweat of Zumba and disappointment.

It was going to be a late night of work to cover the meeting and then write it up for Your U.P. News so I'd decided to do some work at home for the morning.

I was exiting my shower, still dripping wet and wrapped in a towel when I crashed straight into Grady.

"Whoa!" He caught me before I hit the floor and I struggled mightily to keep my bits inside the towel.

"Sorry. I didn't expect you home!" Our collision had also dislodged a tool box from his hands. Tools had slid across the floor.

"Late night tonight." I was pretty sure I was blushing from my cheeks to my toes.

"Here," Grady offered a hand to help me weave around the mess that was now on the floor.

"No, it's okay. I'm okay, I'm just going to get some clothes on."

"Shame." Grady said and turned, thank God, to focus on collecting his stuff.

I had forgotten that the man would be in the house for the next phase of my home renovation. As I slipped into my bedroom, Agnes walked by and sniffed.

"*Smooth.*" She said and left me to my blushing, dripping, and wondering just what Grady meant by his flirting.

I got dressed and found Grady in my kitchen.

"Sorry again, for surprising you."

"Forget about it. I had Zumba, I was a sweaty mess."

"Well it's working," Grady said and offered me a cup from my own cupboard. He poured me some coffee. An abrupt subject change was in order if I had any hope of maintaining any cool, whatsoever.

"Body by Pauline, thanks."

"I'm glad I ran into you." I swore there were two meanings there.

"Alright. Enough with the flirting. I can't keep up." Despite myself I smiled at Grady. He was fun to be with. After my recent colossal relationship collapse that played out on live television it did help my confidence to know that maybe someday, far in the future, I might date.

Ugh. Date. Moving on.

"After Yule, the boys and I will be full time at the logging operation."

"It's ready to go?"

"Pretty much. We've got a camp setup for a good crew to bunk up there, a kitchen, and a good set of men ready to cut, process, and drive. We're not going to be full out this year, but we'll get a good start."

The local high school mascot was The Loggers. The logging business was huge in this area over one hundred years ago. Until all the trees were gone. For my lifetime and even my parents', re-forestation was the goal for the Upper Peninsula. It had worked, like crazy, and the land was lush with trees. More trees than most people could imagine, more than most had ever seen, as far as the eye could reach. Now there were plans in place to keep it that way.

The logging business today would be bound by specific rules. Responsible forestry management were the watch words.

I wondered how state regulations and Yooper Naturals melded.

"Are all the loggers, uh, werewolves?"

"My crew is."

"But I have you until Yule," I said.

"Honey you have me whenever you want me, but as far as home improvement, I'm going to hand off to a few guys I trust though after next week. Like for the upstairs? I've got to supervise out at the logging camp. Especially as we start up."

"Honey? You're impossible."

"So I hear. Hey, thanks for the help with Craddock."

"He's a good boy."

"Thanks. Now about the home improvements. How about the boys and I tear out your cabinets, refinish that kitchen floor, and put up some new ones for you? We can do that in no time. And then things will look pretty good on the first floor before I move on."

"Uh, okay." I hadn't begun to figure out what I wanted in the kitchen.

"Don't worry, we'll put up plain oak, unfinished. We won't paint them until after Agnes decides what color they should be." I laughed at that observation. Grady was now under the supervision of my home décor consultant slash house cat.

"Okay, I have some research to do before I head out for my stories today. I'm going to plant myself in the library."

"Sounds good."

"Grady, thank you for helping me do this. It's been nice having you, and your crew around." It was nice. I was used to a little domestic chaos. Peace and quiet could sometimes be lonely. Grady and crew had provided a welcome level of ruckus.

"My pleasure, and like I said, you should spend more time with me, and less time with vamps. They're weird."

"Yeah found that out. One of them attacked Fawn's receptionist."

"What?"

"Yeah," I told Grady the story. His light demeanor shifted to dangerous. His jaw clenched when I let him know that it was the same vampire that tried to bite me.

"Brule is going to hear from me." He said more to himself than to me.

"Look, I'm fine. Savanah is recovering. Though, the price of that recovery is high I hear."

"Rogue vampire? That's not fine," Grady's eyes shifted from warm hazel to something, wolf like. I had misjudged how close to the surface his animal self was. I was several centuries behind on the history of animosity between vampire and shifter.

"Well, he says he's working on it."

"Too late," he said, and I watched the veins become more prominent in his neck. I decided to change the subject. I was afraid he might shift into something furry, fangy, and not suitable for the indoors if he got too angry.

"My issue today is the travelers. They're camped out at the McGowan place. And it looks like some guy who calls himself their king, Giles Faa? Anyway, he's helping Ridge Schutte spread rumors about Candy's campaign." Grady refocused on me and what I'd just said.

"While a rogue baby vampire is dangerous, Faa is no one to mess with. He's worse in a lot of ways. Did you go meet the travelers alone?"

"Yes. I mean I didn't set out to go meet him. And I'm not messing with him. I'm trying to figure out why he has a deal with Ridge."

"Giles Faa will and has made deals with the devil to further his ends."

"Great."

"Promise me you'll be more careful." I'd had my fill of dire warnings and overprotective males for one day.

"Sorry, no can do. I'm a reporter and I go where the story is." I was a grown woman. A mother. A professional. I was very tired of being told what to do. It was nice that Grady was worried about me. Brule had been too. But I had a job to do. I wasn't going to tiptoe around to do it. Though I would be foolish to underestimate the powers that ran through Widow's Bay I had powers of my own. And it was time I started using them to help Widow's Bay. I was tired of being careful not to misstep.

Living in fear of making a mistake was almost as bad as living in fear. I was done with that. I set my jaw and my shoulders in the face of the latest alpha male pronouncement.

Grady saw it right away.

"You're a stubborn woman."

"Thanks. And be sure to leave an invoice for the dining room. I'm a stubborn woman who likes to live debt free." I picked up my coffee cup and walked to the den. I had research to do and several stories that were calling my name. As much as I liked Grady and Brule it wasn't up to them to protect me nor to stop me from doing what I loved.

This was a freeing thought.

I attacked my research with a new purpose and gusto. I checked in with Justin and he agreed my story for the day was easily the town hall meeting tonight.

Candy had texted me the public ordinance number that did, in fact, require a public comment for a permit to be issued if a company wanted to take water from a local well.

I determined the amount of water that a company like Pure-Liquid wanted was almost more than I could visualize. Since I'd heard residents in Traverse City had shot down a request by the company to tap into a spring there, I perused the Traverse City Record-Eagle newspaper for articles.

I discovered that the company requested a permit to pump

400 gallons a minute there. I couldn't even conceive how much that was.

Next, I visited the online calendar for the local office of the Department of Environmental Quality. There were no meetings listed about the PureLiquid plan in Widow's Bay.

Getting a real person on the phone from the state capital was the next step.

After several phone calls, several hours of being on hold, and several disconnections, I wound up on the telephone with Rupert SanGregory.

"Hello, yes, I'm Marzie Nowak, a reporter for Your U.P. News."

"How can I help you?"

"PureLiquid, Inc. claims you have authorized a permit to remove up to 400 gallons of water a minute from a spring in Northeast Chippewa County."

"I don't recall. You have to understand that I do dozens of forms and permits and documents and studies a day."

"I'm sure you do, but you couldn't possibly forget if you allowed a company to remove so much from a local community." There was a pause.

"Let me look this up. Hold on a moment Miss Nowak. I can't recall." It was annoying, and odd, that he couldn't recall something that could have a huge impact on our county. Apparently if it didn't affect the bureaucrat it wasn't worth too much head space.

"Sir, if you put me on hold and I don't at least get some sort of answer I'm going to be showing up at your office with a news crew. I'm very persistent and I'm told annoying when I show up in person."

He didn't need to know that these days, my news crew was me, and my smart phone.

"Just searching on the computers. Widow's Bay, Chippewa County, and uh, PureLiquid?"

"Yes owned by ACU, All Continental Unlimited, it could be under that name."

I heard him typing.

"Ah, yes, there it is. All buttoned up. Earl McGowan, property owner signed off on it, yes, all is in order."

"Does that change if McGowan is dead?"

"I think, the rights are in perpetuity. I'll have to look that up."

Since there was no will, as of yet, I had no idea who the land would go to if there was no will.

"What about the public commentary?"

"Excuse me?"

"Didn't you need a public commentary?"

"I don't remember, hmm." The line started breaking up.

"Mr. SanGregory when was the public commentary?"

"Here, says right here it was held, at uh, your municipal building, and there were no objections of note." The line went dead.

Rupert SanGregory had ended the call whether I liked it or not.

I sat back. The permit was legitimate, it was signed by Earl McGowan, and at some point there was some sort of meeting. When they tried it in Traverse City over 80,000 comments, letters, emails and statements were made. But here, not a peep. I found that mystifying.

I flipped through the calendar of events in Widow's Bay. If I couldn't find the meeting listed on the state calendar, now that I know SanGregory said it was held at The Barrel, I could look there.

And there it was, a public commentary meeting, the room was reserved, just like SanGregory had said.

It was so odd. A meeting of huge importance that I missed. Not that I was perfect or didn't miss a story now and then, but this was just weird. It would have been right after I'd gotten to town.

Did I miss it because I was so new? I totally would have

covered this story. It seemed impossible that Candy didn't go either. Or Ridge Schutte.

Earl McGowan was on record giving away water rights to an out of town corporation.

And that corporation had been taking the water for a few weeks.

It explained why the pond was low all of a sudden. But still, how did no one know?

The meeting tonight could be very interesting.

The council was to hear final reports from Yule Days planners. The open commentary today would be where citizens who'd read my story would be able to pipe up.

Working the phones and checking on background had taken me most of the afternoon. It was nearly time to get over to the Widow's Bay Government Center building for the story.

But before I did, I wanted to check on Savanah.

I popped in on Grady and his crew who had turned my kitchen from an old fashioned one that needed updating to a war zone.

"I hope you're happy," Agnes said as she and Bubba crossed my path to get a closer look at the destruction.

"I promise it's darkest before the dawn," Grady said. He was covered in drywall dust. His two assistants, Finn and Braden, weren't much better.

"I'm headed to the council meeting. Uh, what next in here?"

"Tomorrow is all about the install," Grady said, and I shook my head in disbelief.

"You're fast."

"We need to be, like I said, starting next week it's out to the logging camp full time."

"I'm headed to check on Savanah at the vet clinic, so lock up when you go, okay?"

"Hey Boss, did you need me to pick up Craddock in town? Maybe Miss Nowak can give me a ride in? We'll run out to the camp after." Finn, the bearded older brother of the two, asked.

"That would be perfect, the kid could use some running if you don't mind, Marzie? Craddock's staying at the aftercare." The two exchanged a look, and then they both looked at me. I had no idea what that was about.

"No problem at all." Grady went back to work destroying things in my kitchen.

Finn and I loaded into my Wrangler.

"Cool Jeep," he said. I was glad, at times like this, neatness wasn't an issue. Finn's drywall dust was falling off in my car.

"Thanks. So, running -- can you explain that?" I asked. Finn looked at me with thoughtful brown eyes. He and his brother may be hotheads, but they were young, passionate, and reminded me of my own college aged sons.

As we drove downtown, Finn explained running.

"A little shifter wolf needs to get the wiggles out you know?" He smiled, and his looks turned from handsome to heart throb. The young ladies of Widow's Bay were going to be very happy when the logging operation was full speed if they all looked like Finn and Braden.

"Oh, I don't think that's exclusive to little shifters," I remembered the futility of trying to keep my boys still in libraries, churches, and schools for the first ten years of their lives.

"Do you want me to drop you at the aftercare?" I asked Finn.

"No, I can just walk, I'm not too much older than Craddock where a little running doesn't hurt me either."

"But, it would be no trouble." I saw Finn shift in the seat and he looked visibly uncomfortable, like he was trying to lie, and decided against it.

"Look, Grady insists that I see you inside the vet clinic. He's uh, concerned but didn't want to make it obvious that I was supposed to see you inside."

"Well, that's a big fail."

"I'm a terrible liar. I figure I walk you in, be sure you're all set and that way I don't catch hell from Grady."

"Well, however will I get from the clinic to the Government Center building in one piece?"

"I pretty much do what Grady says, and he said to make sure you get safely in the clinic."

"He said all that? I didn't hear that conversation."

"Head to head ma'am."

"Sure, of course."

I parked at the front of Fawn's clinic, and we walked in. As we walked, I noticed Finn looking all around. Like he expected a blindside attack from the parking lot.

Fawn's waiting room was empty, and Tyler was closing up.

"Hi, Ms. Nowak."

"Hi, Tyler. How's the day been?"

"Not bad, a lot of cancellations, so that's good. Fawn's been pretty busy with Savanah, and I have no clue how to use this appointment software."

"Well, I'm sure they appreciate you pitching in where you could. I'm just going to..." I was about to explain myself to Tyler when Finn slipped past him and down the hall.

"Uh, ma'am?"

"Don't worry about it. He's with me." I hustled passed the desk and back toward the exam rooms on Finn's tail. Before I could catch up to him, he'd found the room where Savanah was resting.

If you've ever seen a pointer type dog, where they stand still with their face, body, and entire life force directed at something, that's what Finn looked like now in hairy human form.

"Who is this?" He asked me.

"Savanah, she's recovering from, uh, well, a vampire nearly drained her."

"Which vampire?"

"I don't know his name."

Finn walked into the room and kneeled next to Savanah, who

had been sleeping. Her eyes opened. I would expect that waking up to a strange man next to you would be disconcerting. Especially since the last stranger she'd encountered had nearly sucked the life out of her.

"Who hurt you?" Savanah looked into Finn's eyes. She didn't say anything, but something was passing between them. She searched his face, and I felt the temperature in the room get hotter.

"Okay, uh, maybe she needs to rest some more? Savanah has been through a lot you know, in the last few days."

"Yes. She does." Finn stood up, but still, the two of them stared at each other. I didn't know if Savanah wanted me to intervene, but my maternal instincts kicked in. Whatever this was Savanah didn't have the strength for it right now. She also had a lot to learn about what happened to her and how she'd survived it.

Crushing on an undeniably hot young werewolf would complicate matters in her suddenly complicated life.

"Thanks for walking me in." I herded Finn's large frame toward the door where Fawn was now sensing there was something odd happening. It was a high school dance on steroids or something. The two continued to lock eyes as though they were the only two people on the planet.

"Savanah, I will find that vampire." Finn made a vow that sounded serious as heck, totally opposite of the relaxed, open demeanor he'd shown when we were driving to the clinic.

"Don't you have to get Craddock? Grady will be expecting you two." I tried to bring Finn back to earth.

"Yes, yes I do. I will see you again Savanah." Slowly, finally, Finn walked away, backward, as if breaking eye contact would kill him.

Fawn looked at me, and I shrugged.

"Can they be in heat?" I asked her, hoping her veterinarian training extended to werewolves. She gave me a shrug in response.

"Savanah, sorry about that."

"Sorry? That was the hottest guy I've ever seen in my entire life. Like ever." I wiped my hand over my face. We didn't have time for lust at first sight right now.

"We need to talk, now that you're awake," Fawn said and brought a glass of water to Savanah.

"Do you remember anything? What happened?"

"No, not really, except this dark-haired guy, I think he broke the window, he looked college aged maybe, cool jacket on, well then he grabbed me. I couldn't get away from him." Savanah got paler, her hands clenched into tight fists around the edge of the sheet that covered her. I wanted her to come back to the present, there wasn't anything good about remembering how she almost died.

"Do you know how you got better? What happened then?" I asked her, the idea that she'd sucked blood might be as shocking as being attacked.

"No, but I supposed your Brule guy helped. I do have a memory of him around here." I supposed that was good, she didn't have any weird memories of taking a bloody big gulp. I did, but hey, weird memories were now racking up left and right in my life.

"Yes, you might hear him a little, or something like that, in your head." I had no real idea what type of connection Brule would now have with Savanah, but we needed to try to prepare her for whatever Yooper Natural strangeness was on the way.

"Oh yeah, he already was in there, I think something about Beware of the Dogs?"

She seemed unfazed by the shift in her life. As usual, I had the most difficulty with the magical. Others embraced and rolled with it. Maybe it was easier for the younger set?

"There's one more thing." I looked at Fawn and she back at me. This next condition could be devastating if Savanah had ideas about her future that was bigger than Widow's Bay.

"Honey, Brule says you're going to have to stay in Widow's Bay."

"Well, I live here, so that's not a biggie."

"No, forever, I don't think you can leave, ever." I was blunt about it. She needed to understand the price we'd forced her to pay without being able to ask her about it.

"It was the only way to save you. You'd lost a lot of blood, from that attack," Fawn said.

"What will happen if I leave?" Savanah asked us both.

"I, uh, well I don't know," I said. On the one hand, I wished I could tell her more, and on the other, I was grateful that I couldn't.

For the first time, the weight of what had happened seemed to land on the young woman. And a dark shadow crossed her sky blue eyes.

CHAPTER 14

The main city council room at Government Center was packed. The meeting to approve the final preparations for the Yule Days was underway.

Most of the planning had been arranged by Candy. She'd assigned the details of each component of Yule Days to various committees. Candy could organize the largest tasks into agile little task forces, then she harnessed the power of her little teams for her big picture idea. It was inspiring and tiring, and it was all Candy.

The leader of each of these Yule Days committees stepped up to the mic and updated the full City Council on the status of their final preparations.

The Main Street Decorating Committee Chair, Jennifer Stevens, explained how the street lamps would be festooned with garland and lights. She had also arranged for banners at each intersection, listing the various events for the entire weekend.

The Torchlight Mountain Parade Committee chair, who from the looks of it was a vampire, explained the route from Samhain Slopes down the mountain to the town's edge. He drew a verbal picture of how the skiers would look as they descended the mountain each night after the sun went down.

The Alliance of Downtown Businesses, led by Pauline, explained how each Main Street Business would stay open late on Friday and Saturday night of the three-day weekend celebration. Pauline also described some sort of magical scavenger hunt plan whereby each local business and restaurant would have a special token or experience on hand. Tourists could collect the items as they visited.

"Plus, all the restaurants are preparing traveler type food selections for people to order and then walk through downtown with," Pauline was excited about all her ideas. That was what I loved about her.

"And we've all agreed to assist the fairies on whatever improvements they wanted to make to their entryways." Throughout the entire county, fairy doors were springing up outside businesses. Finding them, leaving little treats for the invisible "fairies" was becoming the favorite of tourists who brought their kids to town. I had thought the "fairies" were just creative business owners playing along. Now, well, I would not be surprised if the actual descendants of Tinker Bell were flying around here.

"Hrrmph." Ridge Schutte was the only council member on board who'd voted against turning the town into a tourist destination. He'd frowned as each committee chair explained their progress.

"Did you want to say something, Councilmen Schutte?" Candy interrupted Pauline's presentation.

"It's bad enough we get an influx of Fudge Suckers in the summer to use the lake. Let me state again, on the record, that our infrastructure will not support this Yule event and then the, what's the next one you're planning?"

"Imbolc," Candy offered. I could see her maintaining a

pleasant and neutral expression even though she'd like nothing more than to tell Ridge to kiss off.

"Whatever you call it, in February you're going to do it all again, and we still haven't fixed the traffic light at Main and Birch. What if we get an ice storm? Or a tourist slips and sues us!"

"Let me address a few things, first of all, Fudge Suckers is highly derogatory. We're trying to welcome people to our town, we all benefit when folks patronize our Widow's Bay businesses. And Fudge Suckers is an outdated, offensive way to categorize people who enjoy the chocolate treats our confectioners so carefully prepare for them. To address the traffic light, Sheriff Marvin has assured me it will be fixed by the time Yule is underway. And he's also staffing the weekend with twice the officers to maintain safety."

"Money money money, you spend it like it's going out of style," Schutte said.

"The events we plan make money. Widow's Bay's coffers are on the upswing thanks to the All Souls in November. I would think if you read the reports you'd know that."

The two political rivals were gearing up for a back and forth when Mayor Paul Fisk pounded his gavel.

"Keep it to the campaign trail, we've got a lot to cover."

Candy nodded in agreement with the mayor. She was the handpicked successor, no question, but she'd also worked her tail off to take Mayor Fisk's spot when he retired. The special election was to be held in February to replace him, the battle between Candy and Ridge had been contentious from the start.

The committees continued the updates.

The Corner Yule Log Committee was responsible for maintaining the safety of contained bonfires on the street corners to keep people warm. The fires caused some further dissension.

Fire Chief Roy Vasquez took to the microphone to express concern.

"We're used to the cold, maybe it's best that the visitors also get used to it."

Candy spoke up.

"We have to have warming stations, and they'll be properly monitored."

"One idiot with a flask and we could have a disaster on our hands." The fire chief was old school. He wasn't on Candy's page of politically correct public hearing lingo.

"Noted, we'll keep a close eye out for idiots with flasks." Candy smiled, and the crowd laughed with her as she diffused the tension.

The updates finished, and it was time for the next item on the agenda, the open forum for citizen concerns.

This was the real story. This was the reason the Widow's Bay City Council Meeting could likely wind up as the top story on Your U.P. News.

The first citizen stepped up to the mic.

"I'm Ruby Carriss. I live at 1857 Lulu. It seems to me this town is doing all it can to promote the natural beauty, the idea that water can be sold to the highest bidder makes me livid!"

Ruby was my age, maybe a little older, and she was mad as hell.

The sentiment in the room was of complete agreement on that point.

The next person stepped up and had pointed questions for the city council members.

"I'm Donald Mann. Mann is with two ns. My question is, did you make this happen? Are your pockets being lined by PureLiquid? Because this smacks of cronyism!" He directed his anger squarely at Candy.

"I can assure you that the first I heard of this was when it showed up in the Your U.P. News. There is no way I would have signed off on it." Candy answered and Ridge Schutte laughed at her.

"Right, the same woman who is prostituting the town for a ski resort and trying to turn us into some of Celtic Frankenmuth is now trying to keep greedy corporations OUT of Widow's Bay. That's hilarious."

"Ridge Schutte, your campaign of rumors isn't fooling anyone." Candy said, she remained calm. Candy always displayed a temperament of a person I'd be happy to have lead my town. Heck, I'd be fine if she leads a mission to Mars she was that cool under pressure.

"Terry Zeller, I'm over on Birch, 304. If they take our water, do we have less? Do our rates go up?"

The questions and anger kept coming. There were concerns about the water table and wells. The orderly format turned into a free for all. People were shouting and interjecting their issues and talking over one another.

Mayor Fisk pounded his gavel again.

"Here's what we know officially. The document is signed and filed. The paperwork is legitimate. For that to be the case, a public comment period had to be offered. Which it was according to every single record filed on this situation," said the Mayor.

"WHAT?!!!" The assembled town folk were sure as heck that hadn't happened.

They were all convinced, just like I was, that they'd have shown up to protest any sale of local water to an outside company. If they'd known about it.

"So, what? We have no say in this?" Ridge Schutte was now speaking for the people who'd come to protest. Candy saw that and jumped on it. If anyone was going to speak for the people, it would be her. She leaned into the microphone that was in front of her, and each of the members of council.

"I for one am researching all of our options. I've prepared a request to put in front of a judge to stop anything from moving forward until we sort it out. An injunction will stop the water from being removed until we sort it out."

While Ridge had been hot headed and shouting, Candy had taken definite legal action to put a pause on the water situation. I was more impressed by her every day.

Candy's announcement seemed to cool the room down. There was some hope that they could prevent what seemed to most people, a bad idea. A judge could stop PureLiquid until it was sorted out. The council moved to end comments on the matter, for now.

But one final citizen wanted to address the meeting.

Danny Jeff Soady stepped up to the microphone. I heard several groans from the audience as his appearance.

"Daniel Jeff Soady here, currently between permanent residences, staying at my mother's you know, she's been feeling poorly. Her diabetes is making it so she can't feel her left foot. She went to store last week, fell, broke the ankle. Now she's laid up."

"Danny Jeff, so sorry about your mom. I'll send a dinner over tomorrow, so she doesn't have to cook. I can get the Meal Chain Train going, what a week? Two?" Candy stepped in and cut off a story that was likely going to take quite a while to finish. And she did it with style. The Meal Chain Train was the amazing way families signed up to make dinner for other families in need in Widow's Bay. Whether it was a new baby or an old case of diabetes that caused the need.

"A week should do it."

"Okay, Meal Chain Train is rolling in your direction. Now your issue for council?"

"I move to fund a large-scale initiative to make Widow's Bay home of Plaidurday."

The assembled citizens shifted in their seats. I also saw a few rolling eyes.

"You know we voted on this back when we were deciding to institute the festivals," Mayor said.

Plaidurday, an unofficial Upper Peninsula holiday officially observed on the first Friday in October. On Plaidurday Yoopers celebrate our birthrite to wear plaid for every occasion.

"Iron Mountain, Manistique, even Escanaba, they're all saying they invented it. We know we did. They stole it! We are on the wrong side of history if we don't change the town slogan to Home of Plaidurday."

"Noted, Danny Jeff, just like it was last month, and the month before that, and the month before that," Mayor said. I had apparently missed another huge story, Daniel Jeff Soady's crusade to claim Plaidurday for Chippewa County and vanquish Escanaba and the like from absconding with credit for the tradition.

The crowd started to disperse as Danny Jeff, undaunted, continued to make his argument, outlining the salient points, and momentous events in Plaidurday History.

"Yes, thank you, Danny Jeff, time's up, and we need to adjourn some time before Memorial Day." Mayor Fisk's patience with the citizenry of Widow's Bay was running thin. I hoped he could make it to his retirement party without telling the voters to kiss his keister.

I had plenty now to write my story.

When Candy finished talking to the dozens of individual citizens who had complaints, requests for favors, and the million demands she probably got all day long, I finally was able to get close to her.

"You did amazing tonight, totally took action, kept your cool. Very impressive."

"Yeah, well half the room thinks Ridge Schutte's their man." Candy looked chic in a camel colored cashmere sweater set and black slacks. She was always several notches above the dress code for every event. Council meetings were no exception.

If she had a mentor in that and it was my Aunt Dorothy. My Aunt joined our conversation. She wore a cobalt blue dress coat over her cobalt blue turtleneck and long gray wool skirt. Aunt Dorothy was always neatly pulled together, just like Candy. Aunt Dorothy though, finished her ensemble with sensible snow boots. She didn't have time to be laid up by a broken ankle from high heels, so always had soles with treads to handle the weather. Just like my Jeep.

Aunt Dorothy had quietly listened to the public commentary.

"I agree with Marzie dear, you displayed very professional demeanor in the face of the rabble rousing."

"Thanks, it means a lot coming from both of you." Candy looked tired now that she was talking to us, and not voters.

"I'm surprised Tatum wasn't here," I said. Earl McGowan was her kin, by marriage, I had thought she'd be the most interested on how the water rights had been transferred. Seeing as maybe it would be her family who inherited the whole mess if no will was discovered. I'd been under water on research into the water and I'd forgotten to check in with Tatum today.

"I told her I'd update her. There are some people in town who think she's the one who convinced Earl to sell out," Candy explained to me, and Aunt Dorothy nodded.

"She hardly ever talked to the old man," I replied.

"I think it was good that you kept her away. Her temper is quite a bit worse than the rest of you girls." Aunt Dorothy said. And on that, she was exactly right. Politics required tact and Tatum was as blunt as a sledge hammer.

"So how the heck did this water thing get through? I mean who knows why Earl signed it over, but clearly no one here wanted it," I asked Candy.

"I don't know, none of us saw the meeting on the calendar, every record indicates that it was posted properly, a public comment was offered just like all the rules state," Candy said. I had found the same thing when I did my research.

"Did you think maybe there's something extra at work here?"

Aunt Dorothy piped up again. She phrased it as a question, but it was anything but.

"What are you saying?" I asked her.

"I'm saying it wouldn't take much magic at all for a date on a calendar to be concealed."

"Concealed? How?" Candy chimed in.

"Bibidee Bobidee Blank is one of the easiest spells in the world, I learned it in kindergarten."

"Are you saying the entire town was enchanted or made blind over an event someone wanted us all to ignore?

"No, no, it's incredibly difficult to enchant large groups of people. That's not what I'm talking about. All a person would have to do would be enchant the calendar. Or camouflage it in some way. That's easy as pie."

"Enchant the calendar. Great. I've got Ridge Schutte working with that Giles Faa to spread rumors about me, I've got an enchanted calendar, what next?" Candy's calm was fraying a little, and I felt exactly the same way.

"When's your next coven meeting? The DLC and I will be happy to attend, and we'll help sort some of it out." Aunt Dorothy said it as if we had a formalized meeting schedule for spell casting.

"Fine, call the girls together we'll do it right now," Candy clapped her hands, she would make it so.

"Oh, no Candy honey, way too late for us, let's pick a time before lunch tomorrow. How about at The Broken Spine? A few books I ordered are in stock, and I can kill two birds with one stone."

"Good, we need some expert help Aunt Dorothy. And fast." Candy and Aunt Dorothy hugged.

The veterans were coming in to help the rookies, and there was no doubt in my mind we needed it.

CHAPTER 15

The six members of my coven showed up for lunch at The Broken Spine the next day. There. I said it. Pauline, Candy, Tatum, Fawn, Georgianne and me. We were a coven.

We were disorganized, untrained, and unsure of exactly how we'd be helping our community on any given day with any given spell. But we were united on several points.

We loved Widow's Bay, we loved each other, and we loved our families. We were riding a broom through a tornado, but we were doing it together.

This lunch meeting was set up specifically so The Crones, a term that I no longer saw as derogatory, oddly, could attend and not miss Jeopardy on television that night. You'd think with all their spells and magic they'd learn how to operate a DVR. No such luck.

"I've got tea on, sandwiches made, and the books out," Georgie tapped a pile of books she'd collected on a cart.

"Okay, before they get here let's go over what we know." Candy was ready to lead the lunch like she led one of her committees.

"Ridge has teamed up with a Gypsy King to ruin my campaign," Candy started.

"The Gypsy King AND everyone in town is against the water sale to PureLiquid," I added.

"There is a rogue vampire biting people willy nilly," Pauline added.

"Willy nilly? It's a little more serious than that!" I said and shook my head, while also putting a hand to my own neck which nearly got bit, willy nilly.

"Savanah nearly died," Fawn spoke up.

"Sorry, there's a rogue vampire biting people like a real bastard," Pauline amended.

"Better," Fawn said.

"And my father-in-law may or may not have been murdered."

"Does that about cover it?" Candy asked.

"Oh, Esther cursed Boyd Fairchild with eternal hiccups, and there was a bar fight at Tatum's last night, vamps and wolves again, right?" Pauline added to our list of issues.

"Right."

"Do I want to know why Esther cursed Boyd Fairchild?"

"She had only three parking spaces in front of the restaurant - - you really need to drive around and park in back if it's busy, you know. Boyd keeps parking in one and a half of the spaces with his Chevy Blazer even though he's not getting tacos at the restaurant, just meandering around downtown. She asked him like three times to stop. And then boom, hiccups."

"Does everyone in Widow's Bay have powers?" I knew it was more than just the six of us, and the DLC, and Pam Ulmer, but I had no idea that Esther did. I ate at the place all the time and was clueless! I should have known because her guacamole was straight up magical.

"Looks like most of the women in Widow's Bay, excluding transplants, have some sort of ability. Not everyone's using their talent, but we've all got a little something," Georgie was flipping through a large printout.

As I contemplated the number of women in Widow's Bay that could theoretically curse, conjure, or otherwise circumvent the natural laws of the universe, the Distinguished Ladies Club of Widow's Bay, or Frances, Maxine, and Aunt Dorothy, bustled into The Broken Spine.

"Hello!" Aunt Dorothy broadly greeted us. Georgie rose and locked the door behind them.

"Thought we'd want our lunch undisturbed," she said. The Broken Spine was a massive three story building on the corner of the block. Georgie ran the independent bookstore in the front, and around back, with alley access, it was a deer processing station. When Georgie's husband was alive, he handled the back of the house and she the books, now she did both and hired help during deer season when it got busy. I supposed she could afford to turn away a few customers in the middle of the day.

"How are you all finding your new responsibilities and powers?" Aunt Dorothy asked as though we'd just gotten our driver's license or something.

"Great! But I had a question. Can I ensorcell my yard signs to be more visible than Moran Realty's? I think that would really help me get the leg up. Maybe make them glow or float or have little birds singing around them during open houses." Pauline asked in all seriousness.

"No, oh, no not at all. We're really not supposed to use our powers to enrich our love lives, our bank accounts, or hurt innocent people. You saw what happened to Lottie," Aunt Dorothy said.

"She was murdered by her drug addict nephew, the least magical murder in the world." I piped in on that one.

"True, but before that, she was nasty, alone, and bitter," Aunt Dorothy said.

"It's no way to go through life if you're going to live to be our age. I mean bitter and pushing one-hundred is just a total bummer." Frances added, and Maxine nodded her agreement.

"The woman killed half your husbands, no one wants that in their obituary," Maxine added.

"I've asked Georgianne to run off some copies of our code of conduct pamphlet. It was revised several times, last time being in the 1980s," Aunt Dorothy said, and Georgie passed out a packet of papers to all of us.

"It's not called running off anymore Dot, it's called copying, or printing," Maxine corrected her friend.

"Oh, that's right. So, look. You really should have had this right from the get-go, but I was so busy with the outfits for the All Souls Festival parade, and Lottie's murder, and all our new Yooper Naturals."

"Oh, and I had to give you that home perm too, that took hours," Frances added. Aunt Dorothy put her hand to her hair. Perm?

"After you get caught up we'll talk about this water situation," Aunt Dorothy instructed and pointed to the papers we were now all holding.

"Is this legally binding?" Tatum asked. I suspected she'd like to curse a few destructive drinkers in town based on their behavior at The Frog Toe.

"Legally? Uh, no. Cosmologically though, one-hundred percent. We did it as a pamphlet back then, so it was easy to read. That's why it's in thirds, sorry about that," Aunt Dorothy said without a trace of a smile. It was as close as she'd get to a warning for us to behave, or else.

Widow's Bay Distinguished Ladies Club
Code of Conduct – Ratified by Membership, 1779, Amended 1983.

.   .   .

I LOOKED up from my reading. "You're saying that most of this stuff is over two-hundred years old?"

"Actually over three-hundred, the first agreement got burnt up, and it took us over one-hundred years to agree on the basics. That's a story, you can imagine everyone has an opinion," Frances said.

"But we really jazzed up the language in the 80s, look." Aunt Dorothy said, and I returned to the paper in front of me.

BY LAWS of the Distinguished Ladies Club, Widow's Bay

ARTICLE I – Name

The name of the organization shall be "Widow's Bay Distinguished Ladies Club.", hereinafter also referenced as the DLC.

ARTICLE II - Purpose and Policy

Section 1. PURPOSE. The DLC is an organization of women committed to promoting

voluntarism, developing the potential of women and improving the community through the effective action and leadership of trained witches. Its purpose is exclusively charitable and situationally defense oriented.

Section 2. POLICY. The DLC does not discriminate on the basis of race, creed, religion, or

national origin. The DLC strives in all endeavors to be sensitive to the special needs of our members, Yooper Naturals, and or the differently-abled non-magical.

ARTICLE III - Membership

Section 1. REQUIREMENTS. Women who comply with the requirements of the DLC as stated

in Article III, Section 3, of these Bylaws shall be admitted to new membership. No member shall at any time be a member of more than one coven.

Section 2. CATEGORIES. The categories of membership are as follows:

a. New Member. New Members are those engaged in their first year of membership with the DLC and are active participants in the training established by the DLC to prepare them for effective community magical involvement. New Members are not eligible to vote or hold office. New Members shall be required to complete their training course and make payment of all dues.

b. Active Member. Active members are those who have completed the New Member training and been approved by the leadership. Active members must also make timely payment of all annual dues and fulfill all community commitments and, remain in good standing, as later defined.

c. Elder Member. Elder member has achieved mastery of all levels of witchcraft and have hosted at least three potlucks on behalf of the DLC or approved civic organization.

d. High Priestess (Formerly Crone) – The membership has deemed the term crone as derogatory. A High Priestess will be an inactive in the day to day functions but be involved in the educational activities as mentioned in Section Two.

ADMISSION TO MEMBERSHIP.

a. Eligibility. The League reaches out to women of all races, religion and national origins who

demonstrate the ability to wield powers outside of the known physical and scientific. A prospective new member shall be a minimum of thirty-five (35) years of age on May 31 of the year she is proposed for membership. A prospective new member shall possess an interest in voluntarism, commitment to Widow's Bay, functional knowledge of the Complete Works SALEM WITCH MANIFESTO, mastery of local herbs, plants, and minerals. And be available for community service, and interest in developing her potential for voluntary participation. No additional criteria shall be used.

The Distinguished Ladies Club of Widow's Bay, do hereby agree to conduct ourselves in accordance with the rules and tenants. Failure to do so will result in a warning, and additional transgressions could lead to expulsion and membership revocation.

MISSION: The DLC ongoing mission is to protect all residents, human and extra human.

The DLC is a non-profit entity committed to civic development. Each member of the DLC will choose a month and provide a main dish, a casserole, and dessert for all events supported by our organization.

I READ all I could stand. The document was crammed with voting procedures, provisions, dues, by-laws, and recipes for Jell-O Salad side dishes. It was an enormous document.

"Aunt Dorothy, can you sum this up?" None of us had time to go over the document with a fine-tooth comb.

"Well, fine, we really did spend a lot of time making sure this was all spelled out." Aunt Dorothy was hurt, and for that, I felt bad.

"Yes, but it says here you were also supposed to train us, and we're flying by the seat of our pants here Aunt Dorothy!"

"True, I just didn't think we'd be this age when we could finally pass the torch." I softened. Aunt Dorothy's motivation and the last remnants of her generation did want the best for the town. Even if meant we were all connected to a pact with every creature that ever went bump in the night.

"You say we can't use our powers to make cash, to physically hurt people? Is that the gist?" said Candy, the member or our coven most accustomed to reading documents like the one Dorothy had provided.

"Or get Candy elected?" Pauline asked what we were all thinking about our recent divination of who was rotating the rumor mill.

"You could actually do all of those things. I mean you have the power to, but we'll kick you right out," Maxine said.

"Yeah, we'll Lottie your bum right out. Also, you have to bring covered dishes, that's a deal breaker too. Remember when Jane tried to pass Doritos off as a covered dish," Frances remembered.

"Ladies, the rules are in place because with our power comes responsibility. If we use it for our own love lives, money, or revenge, things become very unpleasant." Aunt Dorothy said.

"And our abilities grow from our connection to the people of this place. Not by hurting it or the people in it." Maxine said.

"Oh, and we enhance each other," Frances started, and Maxine shot her a look.

"It's okay, we can be honest with them," Aunt Dorothy, still the leader of the dwindling DLC said.

"We're getting weaker not because we're older, but because there are only three of us left in the DLC. Officially that is," Frances said. The three older ladies moved closer to each other and joined hands. It was not lost on the rest of us.

"We need to officially join." This time Georgianne spoke up.

"Here, look, ARTICLE 5, section two, paragraph, uh, 7." I looked at the ever-expanding pamphlet. While I had stopped reading, Georgie, who read everything, continued to plow through the Arcanum of the Distinguished Ladies Club.

"Full attainment of powers and magic heretofore described and unlocked by the covenant of Widow's Bay is only achieved when the DLC membership is at a minimum of thirteen witches."

"Thirteen? You're down to three." Fawn stated the obvious on that.

"Even with us, it's not enough," Tatum added.

Dorothy, Maxine, and Frances looked at each other. I felt the weight of decades pass from them to us. There was so much we didn't know. And so much they'd fought to protect. If we loved this piece of the world, it was in no small measure a world they'd created.

I saw love, loss, triumph, and through it, all their hands, clasped. A flash of Elsie, Jane, and even a young Lottie swirled in their heads. I looked at my friends and knew they were seeing it too.

"Look, we're not alone, there's a generation of us. And some of us are going off the rails," Candy said. I remembered Pam Ulmer and her pain at having an empty nest. On her own, she'd manifested her fears into a near disaster for her son.

"We need at least four more," I said. The nine in this room plus four would put the DLC at the magic thirteen.

"Yes, though it might be smart to get seven, just in case since we're all older than dirt," Maxine said.

"Fine, we're going to get seven more women and then we'll do all this, whatever the heck it says in here to become official members of the DLC." I had a hard time believing that just came out of my mouth. I was serious. I was in. The DLC was important to the survival of Widow's Bay, and we were the DLC. Or were about to be.

"Oh, can we get matching sweaters?" Frances clapped her hands in glee as she said it.

"Don't push it," Tatum replied. Her standard t-shirt and leather jacket badass look didn't have room for a cardigan.

"I'm so happy sweetheart. You get the gals, and we'll set up the induction ceremony," Aunt Dorothy was making plans already, I could see that.

"Fine, now we need to deal with the reason for this meeting," Candy said.

"But Dorothy said resurrecting the DLC was the reason for this meeting," Frances looked at Dorothy, and she looked a tad bit sheepishly back at me. Aunt Dorothy had maneuvered us expertly right where she wanted us to be, about to be the next generation of the DLC.

Candy ignored Frances' comment and forged ahead.

"Dorothy mentioned that magic or a spell or something could be used to hide an official meeting. That's an outrage, and it has to be stopped." Nothing could be worse in Candy or Dorothy's world for that matter than hinky-ness surrounding an official meeting.

"Right. Both my research and Candy's shows that, according

to state law, a meeting was on the calendar at Widow's Bay Government Center, but not one person in town showed up, or even knew about it," I explained.

"It's a travesty. The water is life here, for me, my brews, the economy. Selling it makes me want to vomit that some corporation thinks they can buy our natural resources. I'm going to take an ax to PureLiquid's equipment if this doesn't..." Fawn put a hand on a riled-up Tatum's shoulder.

Half the town suspected Tatum of somehow being involved, but she was more incensed than most. I didn't know exactly how her magic brews for The Frog Toe came to be, but I suspected Widow's Bay water was a key component.

"Oh, that, yes, well that's easy to do, I don't know much about computers, but Maxine does," Aunt Dorothy said. I looked at Maxine. One-hundred-year-old Maxine was good with computers?

Maxine placed her giant quilted purse on the checkout counter behind her. She pulled out three different colors of yarn balls, a pair of crochet hooks, and a can of Coke.

"What are you crocheting," Pauline asked politely.

"Oh, I can't crochet for crap, it just keeps people from wanting to steal my Mac," Maxine said, and sure enough she produced the latest high-end Mac laptop from the bottom of her bag.

"She created the first automatic property tax collection system back in, what was that, 1988 or something?"

"1978." Maxine was a computer genius. Of course, she was.

"So, what's the name of this functionary who's supposedly set up the official meeting?" Maxine had opened her laptop and was typing furiously.

"Rupert SanGregory," I said.

"And he's located where?"

"Lansing, officially. He's assigned to our region." Lansing was no less than a five hour drive away on a good weather day. It wasn't unusual for the state to ignore our corner of Michigan. Which was fine by most of the people here, except when it came to road repairs.

"It's always Lansing, politicians. No offense Dot."

"None taken," Dorothy said, and Candy rolled her eyes.

We waited while Maxine typed away and muttered things like, "aha, amateur, cloaking like a neophyte." Frances put her index finger to her lips to keep us all from making any noise or presumably asking any questions. Georgie slowly slid next to Maxine to watch her computer screen.

I supposed if any of us could figure out computer magic and spells it would be Georgie; it was a natural extension of the books she loved.

"Ladies." Maxine indicated to Dorothy and Frances. They slid next to Maxine and Georgie slid out of the way.

"After I hit control-command four it will be go time," Maxine said, and her friends nodded.

Maxine typed the commands into the computer. And then the ladies linked hands again. Maxine said, "Uncloak."

The computer screen blurred and began to swirl. A purple and gold circle started in the center of the screen and spiraled outward to obscure the entire thing.

The three women stayed still as the computer screen then returned to the official calendar of the Department of Environmental Quality.

"There you go. All done," Maxine said and began to log out of her laptop.

"Wait, so what are we seeing here?" Candy asked.

"It was an easy spell, cloaked at the entry point," Maxine explained like we'd get it now after that sentence.

Georgie stepped in.

"If I followed like I think I did someone installed a bug on SanGregory's computer that put the event on all official calendars, as required by law, but made it impossible for anyone to see.

That's why the letter of the law for the water removal went through, and why no one showed up to protest it."

"Did Rupert SanGregory know? Is he the one who hid it?" I asked. Government corruption was a huge story, though I didn't know how I'd explain magical computer cloaks to the readers at large.

"No, I doubt it. He doesn't have any magic. Just look his state photo ID. He's wearing a clip-on tie," Maxine said.

"So, who wanted to sell to PureLiquid? Someone had to help this go through."

"Can you do a spell to see who created the spell?"

"No, I tried to push the sight, nothing doing. The cloak spell was easy enough to detect, but our magic couldn't see who unleashed that bug. Whoever did it was slick. I'll give 'em that." Maxine said and put her items back in her crochet bag.

That was the million-gallon question.

Who benefited from selling our water? The one man who could have answered that question, or profited, was dead.

CHAPTER 16

*O*ur exploratory meeting of the Distinguished Ladies Club had my mind spinning. We went our separate ways with new information and new concern that someone or something from the outside was messing with Widow's Bay.

I wasn't sure where to look next.

I decided a check in with Loof was a good idea. The whole series of events started at that pond and with Earl McGowan. The idea that access to his water had turned the town upside down made murder, in my mind, more likely.

A check in with Mary Jo reminded me that I had committed to recruiting new members for the DLC. She's seen a little magic; that I knew thanks to Candy.

"Afternoon, a little late for your visit."

"Crazy lunch, you wouldn't believe it. Mary Jo, Titus is your youngest right?"

"Yep, I'll be so sad when he goes off to college." This was good news when it came to membership to the DLC. Dorothy had explained that the powers of the members of the DLC were fully realized after the nest emptied out. It wouldn't be too long before we could recruit Mary Jo Navarre.

"When he does, what would you think, about joining the DLC?"

"Do I look like a crone to you?" I could see she was somewhat offended.

"Well no, do I? Anyway, a group of us are reviving it. For the good of the town, it's not just for one-hundred-year-old women. We're going to have a Facebook page and a pub crawl. But you have to be an empty nester to join." I knew Mary Jo had a sister. That's who I was after today.

"Well, Titus has two years to go, but Karen's last one graduated last year, and she's been moping around."

"Any powers?" I said it under my breath.

"Yeah, her and her neighbor successfully completed that HCG diet after their two went off to college. Only five-hundred calories a day for a month! If that's not witchcraft my middle name's not Joanne."

"No kidding, that's worse than the lemon cinnamon cleanse thing."

"Or the Keto thing? I was eating something called a protein bomb three times a day and gained ten pounds." Mary Jo and I commiserated on that one.

"So, how about you just give your sister Karen my number and I'll see if she's interested in the new DLC."

"Will do. Loof's at his desk."

"Thanks."

I knew my way around the office now, and most members of the WBPD were used to me hanging around.

"So, I missed seeing you the last few days." Loof was at his desk, and I knew he was kidding.

"Right, I know I'm a thorn in your side."

"Thanks, Marzie, so let me guess. You're hoping for the latest on the Earl McGowan investigation."

"It's like you're the one with Yooper Natural powers."

"Ha, I wish. I saw one of those bear shifters lift a Chevy Blazer off a kid's mountain bike the other day."

"What? Was anyone hurt?"

"No, some jack bag trying to make a point ran over the bike, parked in front of Esther's. It was about to get heated when this dude just lifted up the car, one handed and used the other hand to give the kid back his bike."

"Wow."

"Yeah, it's good citizenship from the Yooper Naturals that makes this job a pleasure," Loof said it quietly since some of the residents of Widow's Bay knew there was something extra going on, for real, and some just thought it was a show for the tourists.

"Anything new then? On Earl?"

"Earl who?"

"You got several dead Earls?"

"Oh, that Earl. Let me pull my file just so you don't have to call me later today." Loof smiled at his little joke. "How about you ask me what you want to know?"

"No water in the lungs, I knew that. How about the seatbelt situation, I have a few questions about that."

"Nothing was weird about that, but fire away."

"He had a seat belt on, that's what you told me."

Loof looked at his paperwork. "Yep, snug as a bug on that."

"But there were no signs of contusions from the belt. Wouldn't that be odd, if a person crashes and the belt engages there can be some bruising."

"That's true. But it doesn't look like he tried NOT to go into the pond, he slid in there pretty well, the ground didn't show any swerving or dirt ruts from his tires."

"You know Tatum says he never wore his seatbelt, and that beeping thing was disabled in his car. Did you check that?"

"What?"

"You know you can turn off the seatbelt warning in a car, did he have his off?"

"I didn't check that, but if he did why did he have his seatbelt on when he was driving in his driveway?" Loof asked me, and I nodded in agreement.

"You see, I'm not bad at this investigation stuff," I said and pointed to my temple to indicated how much of a genius I was.

"I can send someone out to the car, it's at the junk yard now, can't drive it. But we can try to see if the seatbelt indicator is shut off. That would be something I guess."

"Or not, I get you. I mean maybe he saw the error of his unsafe ways in his final days."

"Maybe, but I'll check it. Thanks, Marzie."

"I gave you a little nugget, anything for me? Just something, like a suspect?" I looked at Loof with the sweetest face I could muster.

"You know if I had suspects, I couldn't tell you the suspects' names. That would be shoddy police work ma'am. But, since you're here, I do have a development to share."

"Yeah?"

"It's not really news worthy, but we did find a will."

"So, you're now going to tell me Tatum gets everything and one of my best friends is a suspect." I raised my eyebrow at Loof. Whispers about Tatum had to have gotten to Loof by now.

"Actually, the opposite. She's off the hook, suspect-wise."

"She was never really a suspect, and you know it. What you got?"

"We found the last will and testament of Earl McGowan."

"Wow! So, what can you tell me?"

"It looks like he left the farm to his neighbor, so there's hope for all of us."

"Hope?"

"They used to fight. I went out there once because Earl hurled a rock at Bernie Lasko's window after he said Lasko encroached on like a half inch of his land or something like that."

"Earl left his farm to Bertrand Lasko. Well, what do you know about that. Lasko had nothing but nice things to say about Earl when I caught up with him."

"Yep. They mended fences and became friends. It is really nice I think."

"Sure is. You know none of this is really a story for me. Got anything else you're working I could do for Your U.P. News? I've got home improvements to pay for at the house. I have to keep the scoops coming."

"Hmm. Let's see, our rookies are going to be all trained up and ready to provide security for the Yule Days, it will be their first official assignment."

"What about the traffic? That appears to be the biggest concern for Councilman Schutte."

"Traffic cops ready to go to provide safety and security for all our guests and merchants. We even have three new squad cars!"

"Are you concerned about nefarious magic and what not?"

"Seems to me that's what the tourists are coming for, nefarious magic and the occasional what not."

"True."

"And fresh powder, oh and the Outhouse Regatta! I'm entered again this year and have a plan to win. Last year our ski split up the middle, and it ruined my chance at the top three."

"The more things change, the more things stay the same around here." The outhouse races were a staple of my youth.

Teams vied to see who could push an outhouse, mounted on skis, down Main Street. The winner earned bragging rights and the highly dubious assurance that if they needed to move a crapper, fast, they could.

"Heck yeah! Tatum's even putting up a new trophy they're going to fill with Frog Toe Wart Lager."

"Cool, well good luck on the race."

"Skill Marzie, the outhouse race is a skill event, not luck."

"And strength, don't think I haven't noticed those arms. Looking good Loof."

"Flattery get you news tips in The D?"

"Sometimes. Any news tips lying around, other than the outhouse?"

"Nope, that's it. Just enjoying a day with no dead bodies."

"Ain't it grand? Thanks for the updates Loof. See you later."

I headed back to the Jeep. I called Tatum.

"Hey, you know they found a will?"

"Yeah, just got the call. In true Earl McGowan fashion, we got diddly and squat."

"Were you expecting more?"

"Not really, Zack wasn't surprised either. Hey, I gotta go, tourists are on the uptick already. We're packed."

I had to give it to Candy, it looked like Yule Days was going to be more popular than All Souls Fest. I had doubts, coming so soon before Christmas, but what did I know.

As for me, I had one loose end after another. The last days of Earl McGowan were still a mystery. Who cloaked the Department of Environment Quality calendar? Why was Giles Faa, the Gypsy King, working with Ridge Schutte to mess up Candy's candidacy? Was it okay to kiss Grady and would he be as good a kisser as Brule?

Whoa, where'd that one come from? I was single. It wasn't a sin to think about. Still, romantic complications were not the best idea right now. I was too busy for it.

The questions I had about the murder, the election, and the water were piling up. They were my focus; handsome Yooper Naturals were complications I didn't need right now!

I had no answers and no story for the day.

Which is when a little more magic entered my day

Mary Jo yelled across the office.

"Loof, there's something going on down at the beach. Two calls, about rocks or something?'

"Rocks?"

"I don't know. Better check it out."

"Just when I thought I could clock out and go home."

"I need a story. I'm going to follow you."

"Suit yourself."

"Code two, Loof."

Code two meant Loof was going to hustle to get to the scene, but he wouldn't need lights or sirens. Which meant I could keep up, but it also meant it might not be much of a story.

I was getting worried that today would be a lot of running around and no new story.

I headed out to the beach on Lake Superior, a safe distance behind Loof.

The sun was setting, and the temperature was dropping.

Justin phoned me while I drove.

"You got nothing so far?"

"I know, a lot of background today, but I just might have something developing. Call you as soon as I know."

"Hurry up, the web traffic is down today. We need something spicy!"

We hung up. I didn't think rocks would be a spicy story but I could hope.

I was so wrong.

CHAPTER 17

I pulled up to the parking area that ran parallel to the beach. In the summer, this would be packed with cars, right now it was a ghost town.

Loof was already walking out onto the shore of Widow's Bay Beach. The beach ran along Lake Superior. It was home to water sports about three months of the year. The rest of the year it was, like now, cold as heck, and windy. The frigid water hid most of the Midwest's shipwrecks under its choppy waves.

Loof had gotten there a good five minutes ahead of me, and I saw him stopped where the public beach ran up to a private dock and a cottage that had been there forever.

Loof shook his head back and forth. There were two men on either side of him. One short, and one tall.

And there were glowing rocks. I swear my jaw dropped open and I gaped at the strange sprinkling on a beach I thought I knew like the back of my hand.

They were dotted among the regular stones on the beach. The rocks glowed orange, like they were lit from the inside. I'd never seen anything like it. If the planet Mars had beaches, they had to look something like this.

"I saw these first. I own the cottage. You tell him to put my rocks down!" The shorter, older man was a native of Widow's Bay, I didn't know his name, but I knew I'd seen him before. And he was telling Loof exactly what to do.

"You can't own the rocks on the beach, or the sun in the sky, or the air." The other man, younger, said to him. He wasn't familiar. Though his argument was similar to Giles Faa's the other day.

"Yeah? You can own water, you can own gold, and I own these rocks!"

A hand full of people gathered around the taller man.

"Look, if you put a black light on them it's insane!" The younger man pointed a light to the rocks, and the sprinkling of glowing rocks turned into dozens. The crowd let a simultaneous and collective "ooh." When the black light hit the beach, it illuminated a silent firework display on the ground.

"Wow, Loof have you ever seen anything like this?"

"No, it's a…"

"Gorgeous." There were now a dozen people watching the stranger shine the black light on the beach.

"They're mine. They're mine!"

"Herb, you're going to have to calm down."

"I am not, this is my beach, this is my cottage, get out of here you all. Get out of here!" Herb, the old timer, started grabbing rocks and shoving them in his pockets.

"Herb, go on up to your cottage, okay?"

"If I see anyone, I mean anyone on my dock I'm well within my rights to shoot them." Loof put his hand to his head.

"You're not going to be shooting anyone. Listen, if any of you all take rocks, do not take it from Herb's stretch of beach, say right here, " Loof marked two lines with his boot, "to right here?"

"He's not the sole owner of this magic." The stranger said. The group surrounding him nodded in agreement.

"Relax, you go walk that way on the beach." Loof was in

command and making sense out of a situation that you didn't train for in police academy.

The taller man and the spectators that appeared to be with him, paused a moment and then did as Loof asked. The man's black light continued to reveal glowing rock after glowing rock. I had no idea what to even ask about this.

"Okay, Loof, you're sure this has never happened before?"

"There have never been evil glowing rocks sprinkled along Widow's Bay Beach, no, pretty sure I would remember that."

"Yeah, me too."

I followed the crowd that was now gathered around the stranger with the black light.

"Excuse me, my name's Marzie Nowak. I'm from Your U.P. News. Can I ask you a few questions?"

"Yes, I need it on record, that's perfect. That idiot thinks he should get credit just because he has a cottage here? That's absurd."

"Just what exactly are you hoping to get credit about?"

"Discovering the Yooperlite!" He said and lifted one of the rocks into the air like it was Simba being presented to the Pridelands. I interrupted his revelry.

"These rocks are Yooperlites?"

"Yes, I came up with the name, it's good isn't it?"

"It is. What's your name? For the story."

"Eric Rayna."

"Eric, you're not from Widow's Bay? How did you know these were here?"

"Rock collecting is my hobby, and metal detecting. I noticed something glowing a few days ago, near Whitefish Point on my regular walk. And I've tracked them up and down the Lake Superior Beaches. I have discovered this, and that man is trying to take that away. He's trying to hoard them and take credit!"

"What are they?"

"I think something like sodalite. It's florescent inside. But with sodalite, you need a black light. With these, the naked eye is enough! I mean my black light helps but you don't need it. And of course, you can see them way better in the dark. I'm starting regular night time tours. This is my first group. Visit my Facebook page to book, can you tell your readers that? Maybe put up a link with your story?"

"Sure. You noticed the light a few days ago, and now you're conducting tours. All in the space of a few days."

"They're incredible. Word of mouth is all it took!" Eric said, and he looked at his tour group.

"Here's a patch of them!" A woman from his tour group said.

"Use my more powerful light." We walked toward where the group had gathered, and Eric pointed his black light where the woman indicated. They were visibly glowing, no doubt, but the minute the black light hit they pulsated. The tour group clapped.

"Wow."

"Now, everyone, one to a customer," The tour group all took one rock each.

"Why now? I grew up here, and we never saw these things," I asked.

"I don't know. That's why I'm doing tours every night. It could end as fast as it started!"

"I guess so." I took a few pictures and then a video of the tour group on their hunt.

"Here, take one, put it in your pocket, you'll be glad you have it! Free of charge."

"Thanks." The rock he handed me was the size of my palm. I turned it around in my hand. It was smooth, and almost warm, even in the cold, even though it was on the frigid beach a second before.

I put it in my coat pocket, and hoped it was harmless, it was probably pure plutonium or something, and I was going to wake up with a third eye growing from my hand.

· · ·

I WALKED OVER TO LOOF.

"So, is Herb settled down?"

"Yeah, I think so. I mean, I don't think he's going to shoot a tour group tonight. I can't guarantee it though."

"No charges I assume."

"No. If I charged the citizens of Widow's Bay for being weird the jail would be full."

"True."

I walked back to my Jeep and blasted the heat. I have determined that being cold is cumulative. It builds up and stores itself in your bones so that even when you're only out a few minutes in the cold it can quickly feel like you stood outside an entire day. I let the warm heat thaw my fingers and toes enough to reanimate them.

And then I texted Justin.

"Glowing rocks on the beach."

A second later I got a return text.

"Is that a new mixed drink?"

"Could be, but no, it's my story." I texted him a picture of the rocks.

"Freaky! Your town is weird. Get it posted ASAP," came the reply.

"Will do." I could envision the brew that Tatum could concoct with the glowing rocks as inspiration.

I wasn't far from my office.

The building was empty now since the business day was done. I decided to go there and write the story. No Agnes, Bubba, or hot contractors to delay the process. I needed to sit at a real desk for a little bit.

I docked my laptop and relished the quiet of the building for a moment. Then I got busy writing. It took less than a half an hour to describe the discovery of the Yooperlite rocks. No doubt it would be another draw for magical tourism once this hit the internet.

My headline was sure to grab at least a few clicks. And the pictures of the strange glowing rocks would garner a few clicks more. Despite spinning my wheels all day, I felt like this story would help me earn my keep at Your U.P. News.

I re-read my headline.

GLOWING *Rocks discovered scattered along Lake Superior Beach*

YEP, that'll grab some eyeballs to the Your U.P. News website.

I closed the laptop and locked up the office.

I was tired. It had been a full day.

On my drive home I noticed a bustle along Main Street.

The Yule Days officially started tomorrow, and merchants were busy as bees with last minute preps and decorations. Lighting, garland, and signage were all being tweaked.

I had to admit I was excited for Candy, for the town, and for the weekend ahead.

When I came home, the house was quiet, mercifully. Not a sign of a wolf, a cat, or my big sweet dog.

I decided this was a good thing.

I flipped on a kitchen light and took a quick look. It was torn to pieces. I hoped Grady and his crew could finish it before he had to leave for the logging operation full time. The current state of things made that look rather ambitious.

I flipped off the light and decided I was too tired for food. Too tired to do laundry, just too tired after the day I had.

But then a strange noise caught my ear.

I walked to the back door and realized it was ajar. I also started to worry that my feline and canine roomies were nowhere to be found. What if they'd got caught outside in all the home improvement melee?

I opened the back door and walked into the yard.

I heard a shrieking noise that ripped a hole in the silence of night.

It was Agnes. I looked around and didn't see her. I didn't see Bubba either.

"RUN BACK IN THE HOUSE!" It was Agnes. I whirled around to see her and Bubba tied to the tree in the back yard.

"What in the?"

Bubba barked, he never barked. I turned to the house to try to do what Agnes told me to do.

But my reactions were too slow. Something pounced on me.

It was familiar.

The damn North Face Vampire was back. He'd pushed me to the ground with a speed that spelled doom for any attempt I could make at running back into my house.

"Who are you? I thought you were told NOT TO FEED!" I tried to act like I spoke for Brule. I slid backwards on my butt as the dark-haired vampire stalked forward toward me. A nasty smile spread across his pale face. I could see the vampire teeth that Brule always took pains to hide in his own face. They were there for a deadly purpose. And they were terrifying.

"He's not my maker. And you ask too many questions." He pounced on me.

I used whatever connection I had as the Liaison to call out to Brule. I screamed help in my mind. I heard Bubba growl and bark.

I was about to be food.

Something made me reach in my coat pocket. I had to fight back. My pulsating veins would be ripped out before my message for help landed. I knew it.

I had the rock, the Yooperlite, nestled there. So that's what I used. I smashed the rock against the side of the vampire's head. The rock struck his temple. Would it be enough for me to get away?

I'd opened a gash above his eye. The North Face Vampire leaned up and away from my throbbing jugular.

"Did you just hit me with a rock? That's just mean, lady." I shook my head at the ridiculousness of the comment.

"You were about to rip my neck open."

"About that." That comment came from behind the vampire that still straddled me. He turned to look. It was Brule. He'd come to the rescue! Well, sort of, after I'd done a good amount to rescue myself.

"I have been looking for you." Brule advanced on North Face Vampire Bro. He stood his ground. They wrestled for a moment, the dark haired, younger vampire scratching and struggling. Brule handled himself with deadly grace that revealed the fact that he'd probably been in more battles than he could count.

The younger vampire charged back at Brule and the two, locked together at each other's necks, hurtled in circles the length of my backyard. White hair and black hair flew through the frigid air. It was almost too fast to register exactly what was happening. Or see who was winning.

I stood up and wondered for a moment if Brule would lose. What then? If the younger vampire won, what was my weapon? Probably only getting in the house could save me. That was why Agnes told me to go inside. Brule was allowed in, I'd invited him, but this North Face younger guy was most assuredly not.

But it was a worry I didn't have to entertain for more than three seconds. Brule's size and clearly superior strength ended the vampire MMA match decisively, abruptly, and before I could even run into the house if it had gone the other way.

Brule was standing with one boot on the neck of the now cowering vampire.

"You, why did you not come when summoned?"

"You're not my master."

Brule cocked his head at the younger vampire and then leaned down. I worked on righting myself as Brule put his fingers on the vampire's chest.

"Ah, now I see." Brule said, I had no idea what he saw. I did notice that the little cut I'd given him with my magic rock was totally healed.

"I thought you said you were going to take care of this tool." I asked Brule, I was feeling a little braver now that I wasn't about to be his midnight snack.

"I did not make him. Nor did any of the Widow's Bay nest."

"Nest? You really call it a nest of vampires? Ew." I didn't like the sound of it.

"I cannot control you young one. But I have finally found you. Take a message back to your maker. If you attempt to harm another person in my territory, under my protection, I will destroy you. And I will come after your maker."

Brule pressed his foot down harder and the vampire made a strangled sound. It looked like he was about to crush the life, or afterlife, right out of him.

"Now go relay my message to your maker."

"He's just as powerful as you, and he won't take orders," the younger vampire said to Brule. Brule kneeled, he put his face close to the younger vampire and whispered in his ear. I strained to hear but couldn't make out what passed between them.

Brule let go and the vampire moved so fast I barely saw it. I felt a cold stale gust of air as he fled.

Brule then turned and swept me up in his arms.

"I have told you not to go out at night." He crushed me into a hug and I struggled to take a deep breath.

"I'm in my own backyard, and he screwed with my pets! My fur babies!"

I wiggled out of Brule's embrace and ran to the tree. Bubba and Agnes were still chained.

"My goodness."

"That vampire lured Bubba with bacon. That's all it took, bacon."

"And you were going to untie him how?" I asked her. Agnes' lone soft spot for Bubba was her weakness.

"I have sharp teeth, don't test me." Agnes bared her teeth at me and then raced to Bubba. She climbed on his back and he seemed relieved to have her there.

"Are you okay Bubba?" I said to Bubba and patted him behind the ears. He licked my hand.

"He's fine, bring us some milk and water when you're done flirting with this one," Agnes ordered. I was going to comply with her demands times ten. I shuddered to think what could have happened to them if Brule hadn't arrived. What might have happened to all of us.

"I'm not flirting. I was worried about you two!" Agnes sniffed at me and the two walked to the pet door that had allowed Bubba to head to the yard without human supervision. I wondered now if we should get rid of that option in their lives. To keep them safe. But both so liked being able to come and go.

"He used your familiar to lure you into the open," Brule said to me.

"It looks like it. He said I ask too many questions."

"Please, let me embrace you once more. The sight of you in his clutches unsettled me. Shook me to my very core."

"You're being dramatic. But. Okay." I was shaken. Brule's arms were strong. Being inside them did make me feel safe. And something else. But I didn't want to think about that.

I had questions.

"You said you'd tell him to knock it off after the attack on Savanah."

"Yes, he eluded me. I could not understand why. I have a connection to all the vampires in my territory. Now I know he is an interloper."

"Do you know who his boss is or whatever you vampires call it?"

"I believe I may. I suspect it could be an old nemesis."

"Your age? So a gabillion years old?"

"That is not a number." Brule, as usual was sarcasm impaired.

"Do I have to worry about that dude anymore or what?"

"He will take my message back. I am going to follow him to be sure he does. That means I'm going to be out range."

"Range? We have a range?"

"Yes, as Liaison I can hear you if I'm in Widow's Bay. I can hear you in the county. But I will be out of it for a time. Be careful. It was smart of you to have that Clach Dearg in your pocket. Keep it. Though understand they only work for a few seconds against my kind. The few seconds were vital tonight."

"What?"

"The Clach Dearg, the red stone you carry."

"These things are like garlic?"

"I suppose yes. It is concerning that they appeared. And now I know that we're under siege."

"What? Siege?"

"There are more of our kind that want inside the sanctuary that Widow's Bay can provide. More than we will allow. That has always been the way. The Clach Dearg can help offer protection, as you saw."

"How do these rocks let you know we're under, uh, siege."

"You would not need them if it were just my nest here in town. If it were just the werewolves and shifters of Widow's Bay, there would be no threat to you."

"I'm sure I don't know what the heck you're talking about. How long will you be, out of range?"

"I hope to return in time for the Yule Days. But tonight I must leave, I must see who is sending untrained vampires into my territory and put a stop to it."

"Right."

"And Marzenna," Brule walked close to me again.

"Yes."

Brule put his hand under my chin and lifted it up. Oh, boy, here it was, he was going to...

And he put a feather light kiss on my lips. I closed my eyes. It took my breath away.

I opened my eyes and Brule was gone.

I picked up my glowing rock of power, the Clach Dearg, and headed inside. I locked the door behind me.

"Milk?"

Siege, Yooperlites, vampire kisses, it was all beside the point if Agnes didn't have her treats.

I had Brule, and this glowing rock to thank that my sweet and sour housemates were okay. I turned it around in my hand. I would need to gather more. Especially if we were going to have to fend off thirsty vampires who didn't belong in town.

I hope Brule stuck it to whoever sent that vampire.

CHAPTER 18

J didn't have time to dwell on my vampire attack.

The first day of the Yule Days weekend was packed with stories for me to cover. It would be an early day and I had no idea when it would be over.

The success of the All Souls Festival had ignited interest in Widow's Bay and the people were pouring in. The news competition was too.

MLive, the television stations from Sault Ste. Marie, and even a reporter for the Detroit Free Press were all looking for stories about our quirky, witchy, magical weekends. Part of me understood Ridge Schutte's concerns about too many people here. It changed the town from sleepy and remote to creepy and popular.

Before I left for the day I found my two odd animals. Bubba was snoring, and Agnes was curled into his fat folds. She however was not sleeping, she was lounging. Lounging was a favorite pastime for Agnes. I still shuddered to think what could have happened if that rogue vampire got hungry and my animals were in the way.

"You should worry, we're very tasty."

"So how did you both wind up outside again?"

"Bubba. The bacon smell lured him and then the vampire chased a squirrel into the yard. Sensory overload for this one."

"'Nuff said. Just make sure Bubba only goes out for critical needs only today so I don't have to worry."

"Don't be crass." Agnes said and returned to her lounging. She would protect Bubba today, of that I had no doubt.

I headed out the door and ran smack into the warm, strong, and good smelling Grady Shook.

"Whoa, sorry Marzie." He had both his hands on my elbows to prevent a full-on hip-breaking crash onto my front walk. Running into Grady was a habit now, one I didn't want to give up, I found, to my surprise.

"No, my fault. It's not even eight and I'm late. I've got a one on one interview with Ridge this morning."

"Okay, well careful driving. Oh, really quick, did Agnes decide on colors?"

"Yes, I taped the cabinet and wall color on the fridge again. If you can get to the appliances. It's sort of uh," I didn't want to say disaster, but it was a disaster.

"Disaster. I can read your mind, see? And I don't have to drink your blood to do it." Grady smiled and it lit up his eyes. I shocked myself that I was so willing to flirt with Grady when I'd not twelve hours ago accepted a kiss from Brule. This, and perimenopausal to boot? I really was positively scandalous!

I wondered briefly how my sons would fit in to this new life of mine when they visited for Christmas. Well, they'd have to roll with it. And they could thank their dad for the upheaval. I was making a new life, not sitting around crying about the old one. I believed they would understand that. I had no idea if they'd understand Yooper Naturals. I'd think about that another time.

"I'll be out all day, if Bubba gets agitated, could you?"

"If there's one thing I know it's how to let the dogs out."

"Any idea on how long this will take? Do you think I need to hire a backup next week?"

"I'm thinking we will be done with the kitchen before Yule Days are over."

"Uh, you're exaggerating. It's not possible."

"Our super natural ability, besides shifting, is cabinet making. We measure once and still only have to cut once. It's something to behold."

I laughed. While Brule was humor-impaired Grady kept me smiling and laughing.

"Okay, I'll hold you to it. Monday morning, I expect this kitchen to pass the most exacting inspection."

"Your Aunt and the DLC?"

"Heck no, Agnes."

"Right, the cat."

"I'm off!"

"Have a good day reporter lady."

Finn and Braden were pulling in as I left. I would have liked to talk to Finn about his interest in Savanah. I wasn't sure if that was a good idea. But I didn't have time to address it this morning. If Grady had me blushing and giggling I could imagine the effect the shifters had on someone who wasn't bitter, jaded, and most assuredly first wife material like myself.

Ridge Schutte was my first appointment of the day. At his request. I couldn't fault him for thinking I was rooting for Candy Hitchcock for Mayor of Widow's Bay. But I'd done all I could think of to be balanced, to include him, to represent every side of their platforms, and to be sure that Your U.P. News wasn't leaning toward Candy.

Justin held me accountable any time he felt something was biased toward Candy and against Ridge.

I arrived at Maggie's Diner early and found Keith Foley there, in the same place I'd found him the other day. I decided to check in with the salesman of all things.

Things had changed in Widow's Bay since word got out about the deal he brokered for the sale of the water.

"Good morning," Keith put his phone down. I happened to notice a little circular pop socket with a Bay Mills Casino logo on it.

"Good morning," he said and looked at me with a forced smile.

"I noticed your phone accessory there. Do you like it? I keep thinking it might be useful since I do a lot of my job with my phone."

"Yeah, I lost one and was annoyed without it. Rely on it now." I made a mental note. I used to ask my kids what the best phone accessories were, they always knew.

"I suppose you saw the coverage of the water sale."

"Yes, it's quite something. Everyone's got an opinion."

"They sure do."

"I guess they should have been to the public commentary then. People love to complain but no one shows up to do their civic duty when it's appropriate, it's a shame."

"Yep, a real shame. Do you still work for PureLiquid?"

"No, just a hired gun so to speak. Their people are in town now, as you saw. They'll make fast work of it."

"Well, that is if there's not an injunction out there. They expect a ruling quickly."

"What?"

"Yeah, city council requested an injunction to stop work out there for a bit until the issue is sorted out."

"There is absolutely nothing to sort out. People may not like it, but Earl signed off and that's that." Keith shifted in his seat. He looked nervous now instead of overly confident, which was my impression of him from our last meeting.

"Hmm, can I ask you a question? On the record."

"What?" The fake friendliness of Keith Foley was now replaced by barely disguised annoyance.

"How much did you get paid to get a deal like that secured for PureLiquid? I mean they stand to make millions. I sure hope it was worth it."

"It was. Now if you'll excuse me." He put a twenty on the table and brushed past me. I watched Keith Foley as he got in a brand-new Cadillac Escalade. If I was going to bet I would say he got paid very well indeed for selling Widow's Bay to the highest bidder. And after doing my research it looked like he was the only one who got paid. The town wasn't going to get one red cent for providing clear spring water to PureLiquid.

I found a booth and ordered some coffee while compiling my list of questions for Ridge Schutte.

Ridge was late. It was now fifteen minutes past when we said we'd meet for the interview. Some politicians were just like that, chronically late to everything. If Ridge did win the mayor's office I expect I had to get used to it.

After twenty minutes I decided to take a walk to his office at the Government Center. If the mountain won't come to the reporter, the reporter would come to the mountain. Sometimes I thought it might be smarter to have my office in the government center building, I was there so much.

City council members all had offices on the fourth floor. The Mayor was a floor above, the top floor, and had a way better view.

It was still rather early and the secretary for the council members wasn't in yet. I walked passed Candy's closed office and wasn't surprised. She'd be running top speed for the entire Yule weekend.

I did not expect to hear what I heard. And I stopped in my tracks. Ridge Schutte was in his office, the door was almost closed, the almost was enough for me to hear an argument underway.

"You're a lying cheat. I paid good money for your services and yet she gains!"

"I was paid to start rumors not fundamentally change your opponent."

"What the hell do you mean by that?"

"I mean your opponent is stunningly beautiful, incredibly smart, hardworking, and has a way with her constituents."

"Why the hell else would I need your help?"

"My services were rendered as promised. You clearly no longer want them. In addition, your opponent, politically speaking, seems to also be on my side which was not your initial pitch, was it?"

"What?"

"You said she'd be on the side of corporations."

"She's bringing outsiders in here left and right. You see that?"

"She's just as opposed to the water sale as I am. In fact, she went to a judge. I think I'm going to go get a few Candy for Mayor campaign buttons. Honestly, thanks to Candy and that tasty little reporter the whole entire town is on my side. So, we're done here."

"You shifty son of a…"

"Now Ridge, swearing is unbecoming for someone who wants to sit in high office."

Holy Toledo. Ridge paid Giles Faa to rumor monger, so Ridge would help keep PureLiquid out. What a waste of money that was. It turned out our little spell was completely accurate. It had showed us what went down. And now I knew why.

The King was leaving the room. I stood my ground.

Giles Faa walked out of the office and looked me straight in the eye. He also smiled. I swear he looked more like he'd eat you alive than any vampire who'd actually tried it with me.

"Ah, the tasty little reporter in the flesh. If you try to quote me on anything you just heard, I'll deny it." Faa winked at me and kept walking with his smooth lounge lizard gait.

I turned and watched him saunter away. There was no time

like the present to knock on Councilman Ridge Schutte's office door.

"Councilman Schutte! Hello? Did you forget our coffee date this morning?"

Ridge, red faced, was standing at his office window. He had no idea how long I'd been outside the office or what I'd heard.

"We were supposed to meet at 8:00."

"Yeah? It's after nine. I think I got quite a lot of information though."

"Whatever you think you heard you're wrong."

"Is it true you paid outside agitators to start and spread rumors about your opponent?"

"It is not."

"Didn't you just tell Giles Faa that very thing? I heard you."

"No. You're mistaken."

"Didn't you sign the clean campaign pledge?"

"Miss Nowak, I agreed to have you do a story about my little league coaching, my entry into the outhouse races, and my LONG TIME COMMITTMENT TO PUBLIC SERVICE!"

Spit flew out of his mouth and landed, thankfully, on carpet, not my face.

"You're screaming at me right now, and yet you want me to do a fluff piece on how nice you are?" My calm served to further fluster Ridge Schutte.

"Get out of my office!" I did as he told and walked backwards but kept a cool eye on the councilman.

"If you calm down we can at least talk about your opposition to..." Ridge Schutte slammed the office door in my face.

My balanced story about Candy's opponent was not happening. But did I have a story here about his dirty campaigning instead?

I walked out of the building and called Justin.

I wasn't sure I had a story. I had clearly heard what I heard.

But I didn't have it on tape. I stood on the steps in front of The Barrel, and I explained it to Justin. He confirmed what I suspected.

"Both of them will deny it right?"

"That's for sure."

"You don't have a paper trail?"

"No, or a recording. I had no idea I was going to be walking into what I walked into."

I couldn't tell Justin that I had seen a vision with my coven of the collusion between the two men. That wasn't proof enough for news and sounded totally crackers.

"So, if you get proof, another witness, a money trail, something than you can pursue it. For now, it's not going to fly."

"Right."

"You have the scent though. If you can find more proof, well, then we have something. But for now, just get us good coverage of the Yule Days. The other media outlets are acting like Widow's Bay is their story."

"On it." If there was one thing I hated it was to be scooped in my own backyard. I'd have to put Ridge Schutte and Giles Faa on the back burner for now. And Justin was right, I'd overheard an argument, I knew Ridge paid Giles, but I couldn't explain that Giles deployed a rumor mongering spell. Further, that would mean the rumors would appear in my story. Even if I explained that they were unsubstantiated rumors, some people would read them as fact. And Ridge Schutte's goal would be achieved.

I had to put it on the back burner and focus on the stories of the day.

I drove downtown to get in position for the first of many events this weekend.

Outhouse racing was about to begin.

Outhouse racing isn't unique to the Upper Peninsula, but almost. And it wasn't new for the Yule Days. In fact, there was a fair amount of arguing about how the outhouse race somehow was sacrilegious during Yule Days. There were several points of contention at the planning meetings until someone rightly mentioned that the Celtic winter holiday festival was already pagan in nature. That Yule pre-dated Christmas and Christmas was better left to Frankenmuth, Michigan. So, the Outhouse Regatta, a staple of Widow's Bay since 1975, was folded into the Yule Days events.

The basic idea isn't complicated. The idea was to push a specially constructed outhouse, mounted on skis, down Main Street. Three pushers were allowed per team. One team at a time had their moment on the track, and the fastest time wins. Any business or family or group of strangers could put together an offering. It wasn't that different than making a float for a parade. Except the outhouse had to be more aerodynamic and include a place for toilet paper.

There were also prizes for best fur hats, best in show, superior team name, and most creative uniform.

The racers were getting ready as Tatum served Frog Toe hot cider to the assembled spectators ready to cheer on the teams this morning. Usually, the event included about ten or fifteen teams. This year the ranks of outhouse racers had swelled. Twenty-five teams would vie for the title of fastest crapper in the north.

I joined Fawn outside of The Broken Spine. Georgie came out and handed us both a steaming cup of hot chocolate.

"A lot of beefier looking racers this year." Georgie pointed out the obvious. The new loggers in town had entered an outhouse named Drop a Log Cabin. Lest you think that was crude, it was competing with The Number Twos, The Runs, Deuce Brothers, and the high minded, The Conference Call.

There was a group of women walking around with t-shirts that read, "The Exhaust Fans." They had pom poms and were ready to root on the racers. I snapped pictures of all of it for coverage on Your U.P. News.

"Candy asked that the teams keep the names cleaner this year, seeing as we have more tourists," Georgie explained this year's new rules of decorum. I nodded and realized that I hadn't seen any outhouse names that needed to be blurred out on a newscast. This was quite fancy, relatively speaking.

"How's Savanah?" I asked Fawn.

"She's okay, I think. A little quiet but physically okay. After what she went through, that's good I think."

The official race began with a trumpet blaring the starting revelry from the Kentucky Derby.

I took pictures, recorded videos of the racers, and generally, I had to admit, enjoyed the show. I was on the clock, covering this for Your U.P. News, which made me feel lucky. This was my job. I was being paid to enjoy the spectacle and the unique culture that thrived in the U.P.

I surveyed the spectators. Almost everyone in Widow's Bay had come out for this first event of the weekend. The school had even scheduled a teacher in service day, so the kids could be off and enjoy the show.

Outhouse team after outhouse team pushed their creative creations over the snow on Main Street. I happened to look across and saw Keith Foley, on his phone as always.

"I wouldn't be surprised if he's taking odds on this thing," Fawn said.

"What do you mean?"

"Oh, my Dad can't help but gossip about the comings and goings at Bay Mills Casino. That Foley is a regular, he was in deep, though he just paid off his debt."

"This is a big deal?"

"Heck yeah, if you don't want to get your legs broken."

"No." I couldn't imagine Fawn's dad, the nicest man in the world breaking any legs.

"Oh, he doesn't do it. But it gets done if you owe and don't pay," Fawn said.

I watched Keith Foley for a moment and then lost him in the crowd. This was new information. Keith Foley wasn't just an opportunistic salesman. He was a gambler. And he was deep in debt to the casino until very recently. Fawn had been occupied with Savanah and I hadn't shared details about Foley with her. Turns out I should have.

It put a new light on my conversations with Foley, and it had my head spinning. I had pegged him as a sales guy, maybe a pushy used car salesman at the worst, but I wondered now. Was Keith Foley desperate?

My mind rehashed what he'd said to me while my friends moved on to our next big mission.

"Any new recruits for the hip young DLC?" Georgie asked.

"I've got a lead on Mary Jo's older sister, Karen, and Pam Ulmer." I hadn't neglected my recruitment plan for the DLC. Pam was excited about the prospect of having a purpose in life. I figured young Seacrest, or Conner, was happy for her to have a purpose too.

"I've got two patients interested, they both have time on their hands and cats, like this one." Fawn pointed to me.

"Great, I've got three customers. With Candy and Pauline on the case we'll double the required coven number in no time."

As she said it the Widow's Bay Police Department's outhouse, The Rest Stop, barreled by with Loof and two younger officers I didn't know sharing the pushing duties.

"GO LOOF GO!" I yelled, and he smiled in my direction.

"I think he's got a crush on you!" Georgie said.

"Ah, no, we work together. Besides, if he doesn't have fangs, I'm not interested."

My two friends pressed me on both sides.

"We're going to need details on this," Fawn said.

"Later ladies. I'm on the clock. I need to go get some interviews and a picture of the winner."

"You're not the only one who has news!" Georgie said, and I was instantly curious. But I had to get going.

I wanted to talk to Keith Foley again. How much did he make from selling those water rights? How hard did he have to push to get Earl to sign? The questions took on a new urgency in light of what I learned from Fawn.

CHAPTER 19

The mind is a funny thing. It files things away. Things you forgot about suddenly take on new significance when fresh information enters the picture.

I was thinking about Keith Foley and that ever present phone.

I had been out to Earl's farm the morning his body was found. I had forgotten, completely, that I had discovered a little plastic disc stuck to my boot. I had chucked it on the floor of my Jeep with the muddy towels. It was nothing, until it was something.

I knew what that disk was now. Or thought I did. I walked quickly to my Jeep and opened the passenger door. The towels and all kinds of flotsam were still on the passenger side floor. The inside of my car was in the same disarray as the inside of my purse these days.

I picked through the towels, separated a wad that had hardened, and there it was. The little disk I'd forgotten about as a piece of debris stuck to my boot was a clue. I was sure of it because now I knew what it was.

It was a phone pop socket. Just like the one Keith Foley had on his phone and liked so much. I'd bet it was Keith's and he'd lost it when he'd been out to Earl's farm, a lot more recently than he'd admitted to.

On that hunch, I decided to go find him and ask a few more questions.

I'd seen him on Main, watching the outhouse races. I headed that way. I crossed the street, to the angry admonition of a few outhouse race officials. Apparently, this was against the rules and completely unsafe.

It didn't take long to find Foley, and as Fawn had predicted, he was on his phone. It sounded like he was placing a bet.

"Yeah, Browns to win."

"Browns to win! I thought you were a Lions fan?" I asked, and he turned.

"Yeah, lock it in." He ended the call.

"Any bets on who wins the Outhouse Regatta?"

"Hey there. We keep running into each other."

"Actually, I was trying to catch up with you. I just had a few more questions. I'm still working on the water sale story."

"I don't know much about it after my part was done. As I've said." Keith Foley smiled without his teeth showing. It was unsettling.

"Is this yours? I found it the other day?" I showed him the muddy pop socket. He didn't answer me.

"Remember, you told me you lost yours? I found it around out at Seewhy Pond." I noticed a visible jaw clench, but Keith Foley remained silent. I pressed on, I would fluster him, overwhelm him with questions in hopes that he'd be pushed into answering at least one of them.

"How much does that pay, getting a farmer to sign over water rights?"

"That's private. How much do you make?" He had responded to my barrage of questions with defensiveness.

"Well, I heard you were able to pay off quite a large debt at the casino so..." I didn't have time to finish the sentence.

Keith Foley grabbed my arm, hard, and hissed into my ear.

"That's a gun in my pocket. I'd move it into the alley if I were you."

Foley hustled me off the sidewalk into the alley that ran between Esther's Authentic Mexican Food and Michigan Ski Bum, the winter outfitter place that had popped up in the last few weeks.

Before I could devise a smart strategy, I was in a dumb position. I was in it, alone, with Keith Foley and his gun. My rapid-fire questions had backed him into a corner. I had underestimated just how dangerous he was.

"Honestly Keith, what do you think you're doing?"

"Shut up, just shut up. I need to think." He kept the gun pointed to me.

"Look, I just wanted to find out more about the deal? For the story. I don't know why you're pointing that at me. It's about the water sale, that's it."

"Everything was fine, this town is fine, we don't need you poking your nose into business deals."

"Earl didn't want to sign, did he? You forced him to sign." It all clicked into place. Earl McGowan wasn't cooperating with Keith Foley. He was financially desperate. He needed that payment from PureLiquid. Thanks to Fawn's bit of town gossip I had insights into exactly what had happened.

"He didn't know what he had."

"You killed him. You killed Earl McGowan to get those water rights. To pay your gambling debt."

"You're very smart. Congratulations. Now I'm going to have to kill you."

"We're in a public place, Keith; that would be stupid."

"I don't know, seems like the crowd is pretty loud. The alley is dark. I take your purse, and it looks like a mugging gone bad. Downside of all the tourism. A bad element has entered Widow's Bay."

His description of his plans put me in near panic mode. It was loud, and no one could see us here. It was also daytime, and I had no hope of summoning Brule out in the sun. Even if he was in range.

I thought of Grady, my house was ten minutes away, even if he was fast, he wasn't faster than the bullet that Keith Foley promised was headed for me.

I had one play to make, and I needed time for it to work. Stalling was my only option right now.

"The police have no clue it was you. None. Pretty amazing actually." I decided to appeal to his vanity. In my head, I reached out for help from my coven. In my head, I screamed for Fawn. She'd heard me when I was in danger from the werewolves, and I hadn't even tried to summon her then. I hoped she would get the message now when I did it on purpose.

"Yeah? Big surprise that Loof and the WBPD are baffled." Keith rolled his eyes in disdain at the local police force.

"That car was exposed faster than you meant right? I mean it was what? Only two weeks? Should have been there for the whole winter. Who knew they'd start taking that water so fast!" I played the hunch that the lower water table was not part of Keith Foley's plan.

"Yeah, whatever, it doesn't matter. One day, one week, one year. I covered my tracks."

"Really you know he never wore his seatbelt, that's another little clue isn't it? How did you do it? He didn't drown."

"The old guy fell asleep, hard, never knew what hit him." Foley had poisoned Earl somehow. Toxicology tests weren't back. I'd have to ask Loof about that. If I survived the next few minutes.

"You drugged him, strapped him in to his truck and pointed it to the pond. And now you're current on your debt? I'm not the only one who knows you were in debt to the Casino, and that you paid it off. You're in big trouble, Loof's a better detective than you think."

"You're the only one asking questions. Trust me." Earl's death might have been labeled suspicious, but it wasn't obviously a murder. Loof and the WBPD had to get the town ready for the influx of the Yule Days.

I worried that Earl's death was lower priority now that the weekend had started. Keith Foley was exactly right; the man wasn't on anyone's radar right now but mine. I decided to lie about that fact to try to save my life. Or at least give Foley something to think about before he pulled the trigger.

"I told a lot of people what I was working on. Your U.P. News has every bit of this story and more. You're going to be caught."

"Shut up." Foley stepped forward. I stepped back. I was out of options. I wondered if my parka had the ability to stop a bullet.

The sounds of the outhouse races would drown the sound of the gun. Music played, people clapped, and the cheering from The Exhaust Fans was high pitched. Foley could pull the trigger, and no one would hear it. I had backed up as far as I could and was literally up against the wall. I reached out for Fawn and Georgie, I knew they were the closest.

Keith Foley was no longer listening to me. He put both of his hands on his gun now. He cocked it. I saw him squeeze the trigger and in that split second, the side door that lead to Esther's swung open with a metallic creaking noise.

My coven burst into the alley between me and Keith Foley.

"HANDS!" Georgianne and Fawn grabbed my hands in theirs. We pushed the thought out together. We'd done it before, time stopped. I saw the bullet spark as it exited the gun. And it stopped.

It was suspended in a beam of sun. Fawn, Georgie, and I, still holding hands, dove to the pavement. The second of time we'd stopped was a crucial one. Time went back to its normal pace, and the bullet whizzed above our heads. It hit the side of the building. Dust from the mortar it had dislodged exploded in a puff.

Before Keith Foley had time to aim at us again, we stood up, together and strode forward toward him.

"What the hell? How the hell?"

"Keith, put that down before you hurt someone," Georgie said.

Keith backed up. His retreat emboldened our advance. He saw there were now three witnesses to his attempt to shoot me. It was his turn to panic. He turned and ran out of the alley.

We followed him. But panic was the right word. Keith Foley didn't look where he was going. He didn't stop to see what was coming. And what was coming was the next, fast moving entrant into the Outhouse Regatta.

Keith's timing was incredibly bad. This year, for the first time, a group of very large, very hairy, very big fans of fish tacos, and new residents of Widow's Bay had entered the Outhouse Regatta. They were making record time. Their entry was sleek, and their ability to push it was on pace for a medal, maybe even a win. They were strong and surprisingly fast.

But there would be no medal for the crew of the Scat Scoot. The bear shifter's entry crashed, full speed, into Keith Foley as he streaked into the path of the fast-moving structure.

To the assembled spectators it was a shocking development and a black mark on the Outhouse Regatta's previously spotless safety record.

CHAPTER 20

I wrote the story about the unfortunate accident during the race.

It was a breaking news push alert for those who had downloaded the Your U.P. News app. I even provided a live report via the Facebook page.

I mentioned I was an eye witness since as a reporter, full disclosure is important.

I didn't mention, in the initial story, that Keith Foley had pulled a gun on me. Or that he tried to kill me when I asked him about the death of Earl McGowan. I could do that in the follow ups.

I did tell Loof all this as they handled the accident scene.

He got to work checking on how much money Keith Foley owed, how he'd paid it back, and on the whereabouts of Keith Foley on the night Earl died.

I was one hundred percent sure all those leads would point to Foley as the murderer of Earl McGowan. I was also 100 percent sure that I'd have the exclusive when it was ready to be reported. I let the competition scramble to find the details on the Outhouse

Regatta accident. They'd come to do a fluff piece on Widow's Bay, but lo and behold, they had blood. Most reporters who'd come here today would see their stories rocketed to their respective front pages.

I filed my story.

The murder of Earl McGowan was going to be a long story to tell. It was wrapped up in the sale of water from Widow's Bay to an outside company. It also involved the approval, pushed through official channels using magic. I wasn't sure how to use that information in my reports.

What was it about that water? What was worth so much that they'd pay Keith enough to want to kill?

They were questions I still needed answers to. But questions that would wait until I could dig further. The idea that there was no longer a possible murderer lurking around put my mind at rest for a little while.

The power of the three witches, in combination, had worked to save my life. We didn't stop a bullet, but we worked together to dodge it.

That part would never make the story. But it would probably be a part of the first meeting of the new DLC. Which if our count was right, would be next week. We easily had 13 members ready to sign up.

It was clearer each day since the gate had been opened that we needed all witches in Widow's Bay on deck. We had issues to deal with that three or six, or nine alone couldn't handle.

It was time though, to focus on the current moment, and my coverage for Your U.P. News. I'd done what I could to solve another murder for Loof and our town. Even though I didn't know I'd be solving a murder when I found that pop socket.

Yule Days had been marred by the outhouse collision, for sure, but it hadn't put a stop to it.

The first night event for Yule Days was hosted at Brule's resort, Samhain Slopes. There'd be a party in town Saturday night, and a concert on Sunday. The town had put too much into the celebration to cancel things because Keith Foley darted into traffic.

Brule had opened his place up for Candy's Yule idea, and the Soiree Committee had handled the night's festivities.

After our drama at the Outhouse Regatta, talking with police, and filing my story, I was tempted to skip out on the evening. But it was a big event, and if MLive had the story but Your U.P. News didn't, I'd never live it down with Justin.

Fawn and I had arranged to get ready for the evening's event at The Broken Spine. It was a formal event. In the U.P. that means our nice jeans and fancier parkas.

"You okay for this? I mean you did nearly get shot today." Fawn asked me with a look of concern in her eyes.

"I didn't get shot today. And the three of us routed evil out of Widow's Bay. I'm actually feeling pretty festive about that."

"Me too!" Georgie chimed in. The three of us set out to Samhain Slopes. I'd rather be with them then alone at home, to rehash my handling of the Keith Foley story.

The dazzling display of magic started as we drove up to the resort. Skiers carrying torches were snaking their way down and then back up the side of the tallest peak. They made a continuous ribbon of fire on the mountainside. It was beautiful, epic, and somehow ancient at the same time.

I knew the actual Yule Soiree would be gorgeous because Pauline had planned it.

As we entered the main event hall of the resort, I couldn't suppress a gasp. Greenery was draped around the beams of the high vaulted ceiling. Flames flickered in oversized metallic chandeliers. The smell of mulled wine, hot breads, and other delicious foods wafted under my nose. The fact that I hadn't eaten anything yet today became an issue as servers walked past with trays.

There had to be over three hundred guests enjoying the food, drink, and live music. But it wasn't just any live music. It was as if Enya and The Dropkick Murphy's had a baby band. Celtic harmonies, a bodhran, an Irish Whistle, and several fiddles filled the hall with a sound that was both modern and ancient. Just like the flaming mountainside.

There were familiar faces, people I saw every day, people who made Widow's Bay home, and there were tourists, enjoying the hybrid music and rustic but warm surroundings. Tatum had agreed to supply the event with a special brew, Yule Ale.

Tatum was busy, as always, at any gathering, but I wanted to catch up with her, for a moment at least.

"I heard you cracked the case." She said as she instructed a server to take a tray of tankards she'd balanced on her shoulder.

"I did. I'm sorry, Earl was murdered by Foley, he admitted it me."

"Sorry? No need. I'm sorry you were in the way of that idiot Foley." Tatum pulled me into a hug.

"What about Zack? Does he know?"

"He does. I promised him I'd swing by the old farmhouse and pick up a few things, keepsakes. Want to go with me tomorrow? Loof gave me the okay before it is transferred to Bertrand Lasko."

"Sounds good. So what magical potion are the unwitting revelers imbibing?" Tatum grabbed a metal tankard and put it in my hand.

"A winter ale, no big effect except it's sure to warm you up. And it keeps you warm for the weekend. People love the look of the U.P., but tourists aren't hardy like we are. This is good for return visitors. Candy and I cooked up the idea."

"Are you sure you're not going to have a bunch of people come with fevers tomorrow?"

"Nah, this is like if you swallowed a hand warmer, except tasty."

"Oh, okay." I took a sip. The liquid went in cool and then as it hit my chest and slid down I felt a little glow inside.

"It's amazing."

"Yes." Tatum and I clinked glasses.

"I'm off. Gotta keep the wait staff moving!" Tatum took off toward the taps which lined one side of the room.

I scanned the crowd and took a few photos for the Your U.P. News.

I also stopped a few revelers for comment.

"This is amazing. I don't want the world to know about it because then it would be overrun! It's our little secret."

"I had no idea the U.P. was so great for skiing. And the food is spectacular. I had a taco today that blew me away."

"Fudge. Yes. And the beer. I've had several flights here that no brewery in the Midwest could rival."

"I know it sounds crazy, but I saw a werewolf. I know I did. He ran alongside us when we were on that cross-county trail."

"You're drunk."

I gathered more than enough quotes for my story. I had the flavor of the events so far. And I had the hard news story with the regatta accident. I started to think I wasn't getting paid enough. Though honestly, I loved the work so much that I still couldn't believe that I didn't have to pay them to let me do it.

I wandered out of the party hall and back to the lobby.

I thought about how close I'd come to getting shot by Keith Foley. The powers or witchcraft that I'd shied away from had saved me, again, thanks to Georgie and Fawn.

The warm mix that Tatum had served me also had the effect of making me a little drowsy. It had been a long day. I had hoped that Brule would be at the soiree if I was being honest. But I didn't see him, I figured he must still be tracking down that other loose end.

Who had sent that idiot vampire to our town?

And why?

And whose magic had helped Keith Foley get the water sold to PureLiquid? There were avenues to run down, leads to chase, but it would have to be tomorrow. I'd reported the heck out of today. I needed to clock out, rest, and attack it all again in the morning.

I decided to head home.

But this day wasn't quite done.

"Hurry, you must!" I heard a voice in my head. It wasn't Fawn or Tatum, or any of my friends.

"She's in danger!"

"Frances?"

"NO THIS IS MAXINE! Meet at Dot's!" Aunt Dorothy's trio of Crones had reached out to me. And they sounded scared.

I drove as fast as I could to my Aunt's. Something was wrong with Aunt Dorothy! I drove as fast as I could to her house, all fatigue gone, replaced with worry over what could possibly have happened to force the Crones to call me for help.

I pulled in to her place. The ten-minute drive had taken me five. I saw both Maxine and Frances holding hands on her front porch.

"What's going on?"

"Hurry give us your hand," Maxine said.

"We haven't been able to reach her all day. We always check in. And there's something barring her door. We need to get in there. And we need three," Frances said.

"Okay, what do you need me to..."

"Think open." We held hands and the word open popped in my mind. I felt a whoosh of air blast through the three of us. I held fast to the two older women.

"Whoa, almost knocked my brassiere off," Frances said as the older women pulled all three of us to the now open front door. We raced through the house.

"Here, she's here, in her room," Maxine led the way.

Aunt Dorothy was in her bed, laying there, but peaceful was not a word I'd use to describe her slumber. She was bleeding from her nose and her hair, normally perfectly set, was wet, and matted to her temples.

"Dot!" Frances said and tried to wake her.

"Let's grab hands, hers too!" I took one hand, Frances another, and Maxine closed the circle.

I didn't know what to think of or what the goal was here. Every other time I'd invoked magic I had some word, or spell, or idea. This time with the more experienced witches I just hoped I could keep up. I hoped I was doing what they needed. They'd traded Dot as their third for me and I was not at all convinced I was up to the task.

I didn't even know what the task was!

Soon I wasn't standing next to the bed, I was somewhere else. I was in a field, there was snow, and there was Brule. He was fighting something unseen. Dot was with him.

I didn't know how I knew but it was clear. Brule and Dorothy were working together to keep something out. They were pushing something away, or maybe trying to erect a barrier?

Something dark was on the other side of the field, a cloud of smoke that had purpose, that had intent, that was evil.

I stood behind Dot and Brule and could feel Frances and Maxine near me as well, we were here but not here. I could see the smoke, the field, and feel the cold wind, but I knew I wasn't really in this place. Maxine and Frances directed their energy, their will, to the dark smoke. I heard them say the word "out," in my head.

The black smoke swirled, it formed a snaking tentacle and reached for Aunt Dorothy. Brule stepped in front of it but it shifted away from him. It circled Aunt Dorothy. Her steely eyes were disappearing in the fog of the evil smoke.

"Again!" I heard Brule say. This time I used every ounce of energy I had and put it into the word.

"Out!" It was my voice, louder than Frances and Maxine, louder than Brule but joined by them just the same.

The smoke that surrounded Aunt Dorothy separated into thousands of little black particles and then fell to her feet.

She took a deep breath and then used her hand to brush it away. The evil force I'd felt disappeared with the smoke. It was the smoke, I guess?

I opened my eyes to find all of us, Maxine, Frances, Dorothy, and now Brule, standing around Dorothy in her room once again.

"What the heck was that?" The two old Crones of the DLC dropped down to Dorothy's bed and smoothed her hair. She opened her eyes and gave us all a weak smile.

"Aunt Dorothy are you okay?"

"Oh, yes, I'm tired, but okay. Did we do it?" She asked Brule.

"Yes, for now." He said to her and she seemed to relax a little.

"Oh good, thank goodness you three showed up. I was getting rather tuckered out," Dorothy said.

"We're here, we'll take good care of you. If I remember correctly bagels and various other carbs are just the thing at a time like this," Frances said and hurried toward Dorothy's kitchen.

"Don't worry love, we're going to take care of your Aunt, she'll be good as new in a day or two," Maxine said.

"What the hell happened?"

"Well, I suspect Brule can tell you the full story, but it was clear she was over taxed. Our combined forces helped. We're just not used to this level anymore." Maxine tried to explain. I only half understood what she was saying.

"Aunt Dorothy, are you okay? What else can I do?" I pushed passed Maxine.

"I'm going to be fine. The girls are here for me now. You and Brule need to talk. I can't do this again. The new DLC needs to be trained." She was saying the same things she always said. But this time I could see the urgency. Whatever she'd just been asked to do was almost more than she could withstand.

"Call me, text me, whatever you need. I'll be back later okay, after you get some rest," I said to her. Maybe I should stay and help them care for her?

"Don't stay, I'm going to nap." I watched as she settled into her bed. This time her head rested lightly on the pillow. Her face was peaceful. Whatever horrible journey she'd been on with Brule was over.

"Let's go." I looked at Brule and indicated we take it outside.

We got to my Jeep and the anger I'd suppressed in front of my aunt and the rest of the DLC exploded.

"What in the heck did you get her into? She's an old lady. She shouldn't be wrestling with smoke monsters or whatever the heck that was!" I really didn't have words for what I'd just seen.

"Yes, I know that now. She assured me we could handle the incursion together. We'd done it before." Brule looked back at my Aunt's house. There was concern in his eyes.

"Incursion? What the heck?"

"The smoke you saw, it was a manifestation of what's trying to get in."

"English Brule, plain, simple English."

"I traveled to Detroit, as I told you, to discover the origin of the vampire who'd attacked you. And that young woman."

"Savanah."

"Yes. It is worse than I feared."

"Great."

"PureLiquid is connected to my mortal enemy."

I rolled my eyes.

"Like you're Batman and he's The Joker?"

"I can turn into a bat but I do not understand, who is joking?"

As usual he had no idea what I was talking about when I made pop culture references.

"Your mortal enemy? Who is it? A vampire hunter? A killer priest?"

"No, a vampire like I am. Thousands of years old. Older than I am."

"Great."

"He wants into Widow's Bay. He always has."

"Why?"

"To steal you, to steal the other witches. To take our water. To take your blood."

"That's a lot." I put my hand up to my forehead and rubbed my eyes.

"He sent the young vampire to spy, he arranged for the functionary's computer to conceal the public meeting, so he could get the water rights. He caused a very large pothole."

"An evil pothole, really?"

"It's a very big pothole."

"Why does he need to do all this? Can't he just come on into town in a pickup truck like the rest of the new residents?"

"He wants more than to live here, he wants to control all of these things we have."

"What do we do? Why did you need my aunt?"

"To block his entrance into the town."

"Which we did?"

"Yes, barely, we would have failed without your help. I know that now. It was a nearly fatal error."

"Fatal for my Aunt thank you very much." It was like I slapped him.

"Yes."

"Well, what now? Is it over? Are we all set? Problem solved."

"No, this was a temporary setback for him. He's waited decades. Obviously, your Aunt and her generation cannot be asked to fight this."

"Great, another job for me?" I could barely handle the jobs I had.

"None of the witches can do this alone."

He said what Aunt Dorothy had said over and over. The witches of Widow's Bay needed to get woke, fast.

"We're re-starting the DLC. First meeting is next week. I guess we need to get cracking. Maybe you can work up a Power Point for us on the history of your nemesis?"

Brule looked at me like I was losing my mind.

I had no idea how many women would show up for our meeting, or what this incursion by Brule's "nemesis" meant. But I did know I couldn't let my Aunt be the one on the front line again. It scared me too much to see her struggle like she had been when we found her.

"I understand your anger and worry. But I must go. I have to be sure that he does not try to send anyone else in this night."

"Uh, sure, leave me out here." Unbelievable, Brule tells me about an evil enemy who wants to take over my town, and then he tells me has to go? My head was spinning with all I'd seen and heard today.

"Get in your vehicle. Keep the Clach Dearg close to you. You will be safe in your home. I will reach out to you soon. And we will strengthen the town's defenses."

"Cool." Brule looked at me. The worry was still etched in his intense blue eyes. I felt slightly guilty for lashing out at him. And even worse that I didn't know exactly what an incursion by his nemesis meant.

"Do not take your safety lightly. This is serious, and I cannot always protect everyone. As you can see with dear Dorothy." There was a hitch in his voice. If some vampires were evil, then some, like this one, had to be good. Brule cared about the town, my aunt, and me.

"Don't worry. I will get right home, and Agnes will scratch out the eyes of anyone who tries to get too close."

Brule smiled at that comment. Aha! Maybe there was hope for his sense of humor.

He pulled me forward, kissed me on the forehead, and was gone in a flash.

And somehow, I was in my Wrangler, doors locked. If something tried to stop me from getting home tonight I'd ram it into the lake.

CHAPTER 21

The stories hit the paper by morning. I'd stayed up all night processing what I'd seen, heard, and experienced.

Man in critical condition after crashing into outhouse race

First night of Yule Days garners rave reviews and tops All Souls Fest attendance

New developments in the death of local farmer

I hadn't reported yet that Earl was murdered. But a lot of conversation with Loof right after Keith Foley was hit in the outhouse race helped me piece together a story that at least suggested there was more to the story of the Scat Scoot running over a pedestrian.

I'd flesh out the story in the coming days as Loof and the WBPD connected all the dots. The good news was that Keith Foley wouldn't be hurting anyone else in his quest to keep his money from PureLiquid. He was in the hospital now and would recover.

For his sake I hope he hadn't spent all his windfall on gambling debts and his Cadillac. He was going to need a lawyer.

I felt good about the information I'd helped unearth. I'd

helped shine light on the sale of water from Widow's Bay. I'd found Earl's killer, and I'd helped Candy ferret out the dirty politics that was slanting the mayor's race. Even if I couldn't report the story of Ridge's deal with the travelers.

There was still a nefarious black smoke monster knocking on the door of Widow's Bay, but for now, we'd locked him out.

I knew there was a larger story about Brule and this enemy as old as he was, and I knew that I had to hear it. But for now, today, this minute, I had a handle on what was what in Widow's Bay.

I had promised Tatum I would visit Earl's with her to collect a few personal items today, so despite the lack of sleep and Yule Day in full swing, I was ready when she picked me up, coffee in hand.

"So, the water rights. Do you think we're good there, now that it's pretty clear Earl never signed that over?" Tatum asked me with concern.

"I think so, I mean the farm isn't yours, but as long as Bertie Lasko just wants to farm I can't see him wanting to deal with corporate trucks and all that. There's plenty as far as I can see for the judge to stop removing water until it is sorted out."

We drove out to the farm and Tatum paused for a second to look at it before we went inside.

"It's a real shame. I mean I don't want the place. But Earl didn't even consider my son in all this. This place would have been nice for him to have as a nest egg."

"He wasn't nice, you said it before."

"So true. Still, it's so sad how it ended for him."

"Yes. Toxicology takes weeks sometimes, but it looks like Keith drugged Earl into a sleep, no pain, and then buckled him into his truck." Tatum shook her head and took a deep breath.

Tatum and I entered his farmhouse. It was cold, dusty, and filled with the things that his late wife had put in the house.

Tatum walked in and looked around. She said she didn't have a specific heirloom or idea of what to save for Zack.

I walked into Earl's dining room, and on the buffet were pictures, dozens of pictures. A smiling Earl and his wife. Tatum and her late husband on their wedding day. And every school picture of Zack, plus the newspaper article of his days on the high school football team.

"Oh my God," she said, and I saw a tear in her eye.

"I guess he did care. It's just so sad that he never seemed to want us here. That he never." Tatum stopped and I put an arm around her. She sniffed, then blinked the tears away as she pulled herself back together. She was not a sentimental person, or one to let tears get in the way of what she had to do. What she had to do today was save something for her son from his grandfather.

Tatum opened up the buffet drawer.

There were old papers and remnants of silverware sets. We pushed things around, looking for I don't know what. Underneath the items was a manila file folder. The folder looked newer by at least a decade than anything else in the place.

Tatum lifted it out of the drawer and opened it.

"Holy," she stopped herself. I looked.

"The Last Will and Testament of Earl McGowan" was printed on the top. We skimmed through the legal lingo.

"You two are trespassing!" We hadn't heard Bertrand Lasko come in, and we both jumped a foot in the air. He was carrying a shotgun and it was aimed at us. This was the very second time in my life that I'd faced down a gun. And in less than 24-hours.

"What do you have that gun pointed at us, old man?" Tatum said. She was angry. I was cautious.

"Step away from each other. I don't need your witchy voodoo woman crap headed my way." The friendly old man demeanor that I'd seen with Lasko in the past was gone.

"Bernie we're just here to get a few mementos for her son, nothing of value, there's no need to be upset."

Tatum had the will in her hands and we both noticed Lasko glance down at it.

Tatum looked at it too. Her eyes widened.

"He left it to Zack. He left this farm to Zack!" Tatum was furious.

"Shut your pie hole girl. It's mine. Legal and proper. That's not valid. I've got a will."

"That's not what this says," Tatum replied.

"Earl left the water rights to that salesman but the land to me and whatever you have there is old, or a forgery."

"I don't think so Bernie. I think you and Keith Foley forced Earl into this. The two of you together. To get what you want," Tatum accused the man who was pointing a gun at us of killing Earl and stealing from her son. I wasn't sure if it was the best idea if we wanted to get out of here alive.

"I think you're exactly right, Tatum." Bertrand Lasko whirled around to find Loof behind him with a gun of his own.

"You see we've got a witness to your scheme!" Behind Loof was Giles Faa.

"Yep, that's the one, I saw this one and Keith Foley in the dark, dragging old Earl to the car," Giles Faa told Loof.

Bernie was on the defensive now. The tables had turned. Loof and Giles backed up the conclusion that Tatum had reached when she saw the will.

"No. It wasn't me, it was Keith that killed Earl. I didn't. You have to believe me. I only helped hide the body."

"Well you sure got quite a payoff, this whole farm, it doubles the size of yours now doesn't it? I should have known Earl would never give you his land. He hated your guts," Tatum said.

"He hated everyone's guts," Bertrand said.

"True, but everyone didn't kill him. Keith Foley did. And you profited from it. You got the land and Foley got the water. And here's a newsflash, Keith Foley said he just hid the body, and you killed old Earl," Loof said. It didn't surprise me that Keith was trying to make deals from his hospital bed. He'd admitted the murder to me but confusing the issue with Bernie made good sense if he hoped to avoid life in prison. Maybe he had lawyered up with some of that PureLiquid cash.

"Now put that shotgun down" Lasko saw he was outnumbered. He could have shot me and Tatum. But not Tatum, me, Loof, and Giles Faa.

Loof put handcuffs on Bertrand Lasko and led him out the front door. This time, we owed not getting shot to Officer Byron DeLoof, instead of magic. I watched as Loof put Lasko in the patrol car.

"Loof's detective work is getting better," Tatum said to me.

"Yeah, and uh, thanks for the assist." I said to Giles.

"No problem, Tatum is it? Let's talk about that water." The Gypsy trained his sparkling eyes on Tatum. Her son was the rightful heir to the land and water. And Tatum's son did what Tatum wanted. This put her in a power position when it came to Earl McGowan's farm and his spring.

Tatum raised an eyebrow at Giles.

"No way Jim Morrison, lizard yourself back to your groupie caravan."

I laughed at Tatum's takedown and so did the King of the Gypsies.

I knew Tatum would never sell out. But Gypsy King didn't know that.

I wasn't about to get in the middle of this negotiation.

NEW DEVELOPMENTS TIE *accident at Outhouse Regatta to farmer's murder*

WIDOW'S BAY, MI - *According to the Widow's Bay Police Department there were major developments in the investigation into the death of a local farmer.*

The developments came to light after Keith Foley, resident of Widow's Bay, was hit by an outhouse during the Outhouse Regatta.

Insiders close to the investigation say Foley is now a suspect in the death of farmer Earl McGowan.

"Our investigation has matched several important elements in the death of Earl McGowan to Keith Foley."

Detective Byron DeLoof said under questioning at the hospital, Foley revealed connections the Earl McGowan case; those developments led to an arrest.

DeLoof confirmed that charges would be filed by early Monday morning against Foley, aged 44, for aggravated murder, and Bertrand Lasko, 73, for conspiracy to commit murder and fraud.

Foley is in custody at the Widow's Bay Hospital while he is treated for injuries sustained in the regatta. They are said to be non-life-threatening.

Meanwhile Lasko is being held in the Widow's Bay Jail.

"We believe we have uncovered a conspiracy to acquire the land and water rights from the McGowan property by nefarious means."

McGowan, 80, owned one of the largest farms in the county. The farm also included access to the Superior Spring. The Superior Spring ignited controversy in the town of Widow's Bay after it was revealed that corporate interests with PureLiquid had begun to pump millions of gallons of water a day out of the area to be bottled and sold.

A spokesperson for PureLiquid issued the following statement.

"We did everything both legally and ethically to source the water in Widow's Bay. It is with great concern that the company hears the news that there may be complications with those water rights. It now appears that the rights were misrepresented to PureLiquid, through no fault of ours or our employees. As such the company has chosen to halt all activity at the site until the investigation is completed."

Council woman Candy Hitchcock had asked a judge to issue an injunction to stop the water removal.

"It looks like none of this water was taken legally. The good news for the people of Widow's Bay is that not one more ounce of our natural

resources will leave our area without complete support and knowledge of our residents," said Hitchcock.

Hitchcock's opponent in the race for mayor, and also a big opponent to the PureLiquid water deal added, "It's a shame that Candy Hitchcock and others were asleep at the switch. Once I'm mayor you will have none of this sort of negligent management."

The suspects are expected to be arraigned Monday and the coroner's report on the death of Earl McGowan may also be released later next week.

"Wow, we're so far ahead of this! Suck it MLive!" Justin said as he read my story.

"I know right?" I had smashed it with this. No other news organization was even close.

"Great job as usual. I better tell Garrett DeWitt that you need a raise."

I hadn't asked for one, but I liked the idea.

"Wow, thanks but..."

"Don't argue. I just have to let him know that the Detroit Free Press is sniffing around his star reporter and he'll cough it up."

"Nice."

"You're off the clock. Have a good rest of the weekend, but Monday."

"Yep, I'll be in court for the arraignments."

We finished the call, and I powered down my computer.

I looked around my little office. I had notes, pictures, interviews, and research, all compiled in the frenzy of the last few days. And I had booking photos now, of two suspects, both who blamed the other in the murder of Earl McGowan.

Loof told me off the record that it was likely McGowan was dosed with Ambien, suffocated, and then loaded into his truck to make it look like an accident.

Foley needed the pay day and Lasko leveraged what he caught Foley doing to get what he always wanted, McGowan's farm.

Both Foley and Lasko were trying to talk themselves out of the more serious charges. But it wasn't working.

I had cracked the investigation wide open with my questions and the clues I'd found. But I hadn't done it alone. This time Loof was right behind me. He'd saved us from Bertrand Lasko. And my little coven was there for me every step of the way.

We may be new at using our powers to protect Widow's Bay, but we had what it took. I felt sure of it for the first time since the job had been laid at our feet.

CHAPTER 22

My first-floor renovation was done. While a lot of people were reveling in Yule festivities on Saturday I'd been putting together the exclusive story on Earl McGowan and the water rights.

But I wasn't the only one working the weekend.

I got home after all the chips fell in the murder story and there was a familiar truck in my driveway.

Grady had promised my kitchen would be done by the end of the weekend. I took a deep breath and walked in.

He was whistling something, and still in the kitchen. There was the smell of fresh paint. I hoped it was a good sign. I entered and could hardly believe my eyes.

The wood floor gleamed and the cabinets were up and looking gorgeous against the paint that Agnes had selected.

"It's like out of a magazine!" I said, and Grady turned to find me nearly jumping up and down like a kid with a new toy.

"Yeah, except you need new appliances. These are looking pretty bad next to the new stuff."

"Minor detail." It really was. The hard work was done. Grady, in less than a week, had fixed my dining room and kitchen. They were transformed. He'd revealed the beauty of the original house that had been concealed under mauve carpet and teal paint. My mother, who never saw an eighties fad she didn't jump on, wouldn't recognize the place.

"I'd be willing to work on that family room area, and the downstairs bath," Grady said.

"I thought you were going to be logging full time starting next week."

"I am, but I like seeing you every day. I could squeeze it in."

Where it was serious and confusing hanging out with Étienne Brule, King of the Michigan Vampires, it was the opposite with Grady and his wolf pack.

"Likewise."

Grady leaned down and opened his cooler.

"Here, have a cold one with me." He stood close and handed me the bottle. I popped it open. We both leaned on my brand-new marble countertops.

"Hey, these had to blow my budget." I ran a hand over the surface.

"I know a guy, and Agnes approved it."

"Ah, well, then we're good."

"I hear you were in quite a pinch, twice. And you didn't call, or text or voodoo mind meld me. I'm highly offended."

"It's hard to remember who's on voodoo speed dial with the fate of the town in the balance every five minutes." I took a drink of the cold beer. I felt some of the stress of the last few days slide away.

Grady laughed at my joke. Something about his laugh, his home improvement skills, and the way he casually leaned against my kitchen counter affected me. I didn't really plan it, or think it through, but I leaned in and planted my lips on his.

I'd meant to land a sweet little flirtatious kiss on his gorgeous face. But my sweet turned into something spicy as he kissed me back and put a hand around my waist. His hand now rested on my hip. This was a lot more familiar than I had planned when I leaned in.

I pulled back and studied the surprised face of Grady Shook.

"If you think that means I'm giving you a discount on refinishing this floor, think again. I have mouths to feed."

"Shut up, no. I…" I was now a bit flustered. My curiosity had just written a check that the rest of me wasn't quite ready to cash.

"I'm hard to get rid of, fair warning." Grady kissed me this time, but it was on my hand. It was a gallant way to get me out of a situation I wasn't ready for yet.

"Great."

He put the beer down, grabbed his cooler and packed up to go.

"I'm sorry I just had to see what it was like."

"Kissing a werewolf? The verdict?"

"Scratchy. But in a good way." He smiled and again I was struck by his rugged good looks.

I walked him to the door. I would also miss coming home to find him working here. I started to think about all the possible future home improvements I needed.

"Sidenote, we're mated for life now, that's how werewolf dating works." Grady said. And panic shot through my throat to my stomach. I had no idea what the rules were for kissing vampires and werewolves.

"What?"

"Kidding, I'm kidding. But you probably do owe me a pizza or something." I shook my head and closed the door on Grady and his hearty laugh.

I turned to see Agnes sauntering by on her way to her new bedding in the dining room.

"Slut."

"It was just a kiss!"

And yes, I was trying to justify kissing a werewolf to my cat.

217

Which really was a typical night, it turned out, in Widow's Bay.

* * *

"Ladies let's be seated." We decided to meet at Tatum's place. The Frog Toe had recently opened a banquet and meeting room. It was perfect for our group.

A table had been set up in the front of the room and two dozen chairs were arranged for the attendees.

"Dear, you need to use that little gavel, or they'll never pipe down." Aunt Dorothy was sitting next to Candy, who'd tried in vain, twice, to start the meeting. Maxine was instructing Georgie how to take proper, official minutes, with some sort of magic iPad app.

"You don't want the whole state knowing our business," she explained as the two hovered over the screen.

Frances and Pauline had brought cookies for everyone to snack on, while Fawn and I were responsible for making sure everyone actually showed up.

We'd been charged with making sure we had 13 women total to restart the club. Which, including the six of us and the old Crones, meant we only needed four new people. But once word got around to the football moms, the soccer moms, the snow mobile club, the bow hunting club, and the Euchre club the numbers swelled.

There were twenty-six witches in attendance. Though only three of our number, the old ones, The Crones, had a clue what it really meant to be a Witch of Widow's Bay.

Even I didn't know my way around a wand, metaphorically speaking, and I'd stopped time and fended off a dark force trying to move in to Chippewa County.

Candy beat the little brass gavel on the banquet table as Aunt Dorothy instructed.

"Ladies! Let's get the meeting underway!" Candy was louder this time and it worked. The assembled group settled down.

"I'm going to turn it over to Dorothy Nurse."

Aunt Dorothy was still weak from her adventure with Brule. And I was still unsure if I forgave him for letting her have that adventure. He still had a lot of explaining to do on how his nemesis was trying to get into Widow's Bay through PureLiquid and its parent company, All Continental Unlimited.

It was enough, for now, that we'd blocked them.

The North Face Vampire had also disappeared. Brule said the young vampire was in hiding, or maybe his maker had killed him? The North Face Vampire had been sent to spy on me and the town. He wound up getting caught and being thoroughly unable to go more than a day without biting someone. As a spy he sucked. He was probably in trouble from his boss.

And Tatum, now in control of Earl McGowan's land and water, via her son, put the halt to any water removal. There was no plan yet, on how to use Earl's farm, but Tatum was content that her son Zack had a legacy, or an inheritance, if he wanted it someday.

Other than the accident at the Outhouse Regatta, Yule Days had been a huge success, no tourists were eaten, and no more pot holes appeared. This felt like a win.

Residents of Widow's Bay were proud of the success of Yule Days and prouder still of the news coverage about our quaint little town. So much so that Candy had volunteers lining up to help plan the next festival, which was on the calendar for February.

Between now and then we had work to do for the new Distinguished Ladies Club. The higher profile we had among tourists also meant we had a higher profile in the supernatural world. Who knew what kind of crowd that would attract?

I was certain that we, the younger women, needed to learn, and learn fast. The memory of that black smoke trying to suffocate Aunt Dorothy had given me nightmares. It wanted in, and we had to be ready the next time it tried. I had learned a lot about shifters, travelers, and vampires in the last few days, but there were still trolls to contend with. A group of them had vandalized Holiday Gas. I had no idea what motivated a troll. But they were moving in, just like the rest of the Yooper Naturals. Which was why this meeting was a necessity.

Aunt Dorothy stood up. She looked taller, stronger, younger even, in this moment, as she spoke to all of us. She'd completely recovered.

"Welcome to the first meeting of the new Widow's Bay Distinguished Ladies Club," My Aunt said, and she was immediately interrupted.

"Isn't that sort of old fashioned, can we call ourselves something else?"

"Yes, and we really need a Facebook group."

"Are we going to do one of those wine and canvas parties? That's a great fundraiser and so fun!"

"Let's skip the canvas part." Another woman chimed in.

"Oh, did you see who Loof is dating, Facebook official?" Another of the ladies chimed in and the meeting, which hadn't even started, was careening out of control.

Aunt Dorothy took the gavel from Candy. She pounded it hard, twice as loud as Candy had. The room went silent.

"Ladies, you are now a part of a club that is centuries old, you are part of a sisterhood that will sustain you through death, depression, and even menopause. You are here because you can wield incredible power. Only women of our strength, in this very room can match the forces that now and once before called Widow's Bay home. This town is in dire need of all of us. Staying in this coven means you will be asked to defend, protect, and battle in the name of our citizens. You're here because your ancestors paved the way and it is your turn now to answer the call!"

All talk of Facebook, fundraising, and who Byron DeLoof took as his partner for his neighborhood progressive dinner stopped. They understood, this was a serious group with an epic mission. Aunt Dorothy's voice was strong, her speech produced goose bumps on my skin. I looked around.

Every witch in the place sat up straight, and hung on Aunt Dorothy's next word.

Mary Jo's sister Karen raised her hand and stood up.

"I'm in. But this better include tips for dating those bear shifters, because, well we all saw that one Pauline almost hit with her car. He was naked. It was impressive." Pauline nodded in agreement at the assessment of the hot bear shifter she nearly accidently ran over.

Candy, standing behind Dorothy, rolled her eyes at the comment.

"Oh of course! I mean that's one of the perks! Also, we've got a great spell that reduces hot flashes." Aunt Dorothy's serious tone evaporated, and she was back to her loveable batty self. The idea that she and the ladies dated Yooper Naturals, back in their day, made me smile.

If these women figured out I'd already kissed a vampire and a werewolf, they'd make me their new president. I decided to keep that to myself lest I'd get elected to something.

"Oh, good, okay, so let's get cracking! Do we get brooms?" Pam Ulmer added.

"That's later, we need to train you on spells first," Maxine answered.

For a moment I thought my head might actually explode.

"So, the first order of business is electing officers!" Aunt Dorothy plowed ahead with the meeting.

Tatum's duties as the host were over for a moment and she came over to sit with Fawn and me.

"Brooms? We were really getting brooms?" I said under my breath to the two of them.

"Can we use Swiffers? I actually like those better," Fawn replied.

"Sure, Swiffers seem better with shifters around, because, I mean shedding," Tatum quipped.

The first meeting of the new Distinguished Ladies Club was underway. In less than one minute we covered dating shifters, hot flashes, and protecting the entire town.

It was pretty similar to the million PTA meetings we'd likely all been to, except for the battling evil forces component.

I wondered if we did get brooms?

Now that I thought about it, flying around town on a broom might be practical. I couldn't think of a better way to avoid evil potholes or hitting a deer.

THE END

UP NEXT - LATE BROOMERS

WIDOW'S BAY BOOK THREE

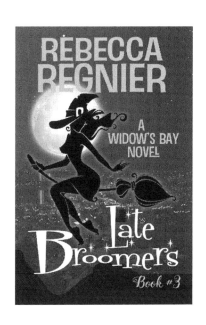

ABOUT THE AUTHOR

Rebecca Regnier is an award winning newspaper columnist and former television news anchor. She lives in Michigan with her husband and sons.
rebeccaregnier.com

facebook.com/RLRegnier

instagram.com/rebeccaregnier

twitter.com/LaughItOff

youtube.com/rebeccaregniertv

Made in the USA
Columbia, SC
25 May 2019